More Than a Moment

Dean Rylah

Contents

Chapter 1

I sighed as I closed the front door to Lee's house behind me, turning to find that he'd already walked ahead and into the lounge. He's not the politest of people. Walking down the hall and past the stairs, to the living room door that Lee had disappeared into, I noticed for the first time all of the photos they had in frames aligning the wall - not that I haven't been here countless times before hand, but I've never really taken in the look of the place.

It was dark since the Towson's loved to save on energy and contribute to saving the planet - well, his mother and father did, Lee on the other hand couldn't really give two shits about conserving energy and his carbon footprint. Not that I could say much towards that, I'm the same.

As I neared the entrance I could hear the conversation they were having.

"Where've you been all afternoon?" I'm pretty sure that was his older sisters voice, Kimberly - I should know, I've had enough fantasies to recognise it. Sometimes it sucks to be young when there's a really hot girl whose two years older than you and thinks that you're still a "kid" - fuck, I'm sixteen, I'm not a child anymore. But she obviously doesn't see that.

"Just hanging with Jake." Lee replied, I just caught him shrug as I swung around the door frame to grace them with my presence as if on cue, with a sweet smile set in my features. I, unlike Lee, am always polite. It pays when you need favours or a place to stay.

"Ah, hello Jake!" Mrs. Towson exclaimed with a warm grin.

"Hey." I stopped by Lee's side who, most likely on purpose, was stood in direct view of the television in order to make sure everyone's attention stayed focused on him. Attention whore. His sister didn't look too happy about that, curled up on the couch with a blanket snuggled around her. I'd join her if their mother wasn't in the room.

"So what did you get up to?" She asked, the grin still fixed in place; flashing bleached teeth with her blue eyes fixed upon her son, stood to my left.

"Nothing really. Hung around with some of Jake's mates and met his girlfriend." I swallowed with embarrassment at that point - I felt like nudging him and saying, not in front of your mum, but I kept my cool even as I sported a faint blush.

With a slight raise of an eyebrow at Lee's little girlfriend comment, his mum asked, "Are you hungry? Do you want something to eat?"

"No, it's okay. We shared a Maccy D's." Lee turned his head to look at me, his hands shoved in his pockets in his usual fashion. "Unless you're still hungry?" His eyes flickered up and down my face as he waited for my answer.

"Nah, I'm fine thanks." Which reminded me; Lee spilt fucking coke on my shirt - which is expensive material and definitely isn't going to please my own mother. With a roll of my eyes and a quick glance at the faded stain on my white shirt, I leaned towards Lee and murmured, "I'll be up in your room." Before shooting a quick smile towards his mother and sister and turning to the doorway once more.

As I left, I faintly heard his mum say something like, "Your father won't be home 'til late tonight, he's got a heavy work load this month." I took the stairs two steps at a time, turning right and heading down the narrow hall to Lee's room. Even though they were quite well off - money wise - they didn't like to make it obvious with a big house and flashy cars. I liked that about them. My parents on the other hand are complete twats, constantly flashing their notes around like it's just a worthless piece of paper.

I swung open the door to Lee's room, closing it quietly behind me.

I've always liked Lee's bedroom; plain and simple with only the things he needs - a double bed in the centre of the floor with a television mounted on the wall in direct line, his x-box laying underneath on the top of his drawers, which is where I once found dirty magazines when we were fourteen...

But my favourite thing in his room was his wardrobe, taking up the entire length of one wall with mirrors for doors - doors that slide open, nonetheless. My wardrobes just a fucking cupboard. And the doors don't even slide.

Approaching said wardrobe, I slid the doors open and flicked through his clothing and resulted in picking out one of the only three shirts he owns. Closing the doors once again, I stripped myself from my top and threw it onto the drawers to remind me to pick them up before leaving. Slipping Lee's, almost identical to my own, shirt over my shoulders buttoning it up slowly, covering my toned abdomen one inch at a time.

Just as I was adjusting the collar and ruffling my brown hair up a bit, Lee sauntered into view. "Is that my shirt?" Was the first words that left his mouth. I turned to face him, smugly.

"You spilt coke on mine, remember? I'll give you it back tomorrow."

"I'm sure you will. If I did a house raid, I'm willing to bet there's like fifty different items of my clothing just in your room, never mind the entire house."

"Well, then you shouldn't forget to take your clothes with you when you stay over." I smirked, walking over to where Lee was leaning against his drawers, beneath his television.

"Mm-hm. Rachel, your girlfriend, bit of a whore don't you think?" Well that came out of no where. I stared at him for few seconds in silence, contemplating how to answer that as I shoved my hands in my pockets and leaned back on the balls of my feet slightly.

"Erm, I guess? She's not really my girlfriend anyway. She sleeps with who she wants too and I sleep with who I want too." I shrugged with nonchalance.

"What kind of relationship is that?" Lee's voice was quiet now, like he was saying a secret.

"I believe it's called an open one."

"And you'd still want to sleep with her after she's been slutting it up with a bunch a lads?" His eyebrows almost shot off his forehead at that, which made me laugh.

"Course not. We don't sleep with each other, she's just good to have around. My connection to connections." I widened my eyes with mock. Lee's eyes trailed down and focused more intently on his shirt that I wore. His stare felt heated and I smirked as he quickly turned his head to the side, to his Ipod hooked up to his speakers and watched as his index tapped the music on.

"You had to pick out my most expensive shirt, didn't you? That was the one that still had the tag on." He spoke quietly with a smile entertaining his lips. I bit the inside of my cheek, cocking one eyebrow.

"It doesn't anymore." Before he could have his bitch fit, I jumped straight in, "Sorry, okay! I'll buy you another. You know I hate t-shirts."

"No, it's fine. I don't care anyway." He paused before, "Hey, where's your tie?" My hands instantly flew to my neck where my tie should be situated. But wasn't.

"Fuck, where've I put it..." I picked up my dirty shirt that lay crumpled on the drawers to my right and found that it wasn't where I'd left it. "Oh shit, that's a fucking expensive tie."

"When is anything you own not expensive, Jake?" His voice was full humor. I jolted my head up to fix him with a hard glare before my eyes caught sight of a silk, silver tie wrapped slightly wrong around Lee's neck. Relaxing, I sighed and closed the distance, waiting patiently for him to hand it back over. He noticed this and answered me with, "A shirt for a tie."

"That tie is way more expensive than this shirt." I pinched the thin material covering my body with my fingers, pulling it away from my stomach as a gesture. I brought my hands up, enclosing my fingers delicately around the knot, slipping it loose and allowing it to slide free from Lee's neck. In return, Lee's right hand flicked open the bottom button on my shirt - his shirt, oh this could get confusing. Let's just say it's my shirt, for now, since I'm the one wearing it.

His fingers didn't stop, swiftly pushing out the plastic, clear buttons from their assigned holes. Our eye contact never broke until there was a quick tug in the middle of the material. A smile flashed across Lee's face as he struggled with undoing the rest of the buttons. I returned the smile with a huff of laughter.

"Fuck. I'm no expert, okay?" He rolled his eyes and allowed his hand to drop back to his side.

"Clearly."

"I was only using one hand." He attempted to justify, pushing me backwards until the backs of my knees hit the edge of his bed and I collapsed down into the mattress, bracing myself with my elbows. He stood over one of my legs with a smug grin.

Just for the rush of arrogance, I pushed myself up into a sitting position and gripped the opening of Lee's jeans between my thumb and index finger before deftly flicking it open. I smiled up at him victoriously as he lowered himself onto the bed, his knees bending and supporting his weight on the small area he balanced on.

I shifted against the knee that pressed against me, in between my legs. A flash of pleasure shot through me, but I didn't show it outwardly. I watched Lee swallow, his brown eyes jumping from his knees position, my lips and my own brown eyes over and over.

Raising my fingertips to his own, I pressed the base of my index against his before trailing my fingers up to his wrist and in one swift, quick movement, pulled him down onto the bed and rolled on top of him.

Straddling his waist, I shifted until I was comfortable, smiling down on him. He arched his back suggestively as his tongue glided wetly across his lips, his breathing upping it's pace.

Biting back a gasp, I watched as Lee undid the rest of my shirts buttons. "Fuck." I muttered nervously, unknowing of where to go from here. It's not like we were... you know, into each other or anything - we just liked to fool around, but it's never gone anywhere serious. This didn't feel quite the same though.

Lee's eyes normally didn't rake over my body with a look of want, the way they're doing now. I started to feel uncomfortable, but I didn't want to get up. Lee's fingers were still playing with the ends of the shirt, causing it to brush against my skin that sent shivers over my body. I just couldn't stop looking-

Three impatient raps on Lee's door before I heard, "Dude, what're you doing in there? Would you open up?" I fucking jumped off Lee so fast, my hands quickly buttoning up my shirt and fixing my tie into place. Turning to make sure I looked presentable and not full of lust. I found Lee had done up his pants again and was looking towards me for reassurance to open the door. I nodded curtly and attempted to look casual as his sister sauntered on into the room with an air of suspicion.

"God, I was knocking on that bloody door for ages." She sighed.

My blood was rushing through my body at a fucking speed I wasn't used to; I felt dizzy. What the fuck was I doing? What the fuck was Lee doing? I shook my head and focused on Kimberly who now lay outstretched on Lee's bed.

"Hey, Kim." Lee greeted, his voice quivering from probably the same reason as why I felt so nervous. If she'd have walked in u nannounced... it would of taken some explaining about why I was straddling her brother like we were making out. Thank God she didn't. I really hope this conversation won't be too awkward.

Chapter 2

Lee shut the door softly, turning to look at me with an obvious look of relief and huffing out a breath he'd been holding since his sister walked in. I returned the same expression, collapsing on one side of his bed; my right leg draping just over the edge. I listened as he shuffled over to join me, falling into the other half of the mattress, his hand touching mine only slightly. Turning my head to look at him, I fidgeted until I found a comfortable position. Lee looked back at me blankly.

"That was close," I muttered into the few inches of space between us. His blonde hair shook gently as he nodded in agreement. An unfamiliar emotion washed through me, my eyes sweeping across his face trying to evaluate my feelings.

"What are we doing, Lee?" My voice lowered to a mere whisper. Lee's eyes found my own, holding my gaze, his eyebrows curved down in confusion.

"What do you mean?" His voice was no louder than mine.

"You know what," I licked my lips and took in a breath. "Us, fooling around and shit. It's gonna' get us caught some day and people won't see it the way we do."

"How do you see it?" The question came with surprise on my behalf, taking me a moment to understand.

"How do you?" I blocked, pushing the spotlight onto Lee instead. He rolled his eyes at me before cocking an eyebrow.

"I asked first." There was a moment of silence whilst we stared at each other before we both huffed out a breathy laugh and slid our gaze up to the ceiling. I stayed quiet though, I wasn't about to make the first move into the uncomfortable discussion of our feelings. That isn't territory I'm familiar with, for a start.

"Okay, I see it as just us being...us, really. I mean, you've always been a bit camp, dude." I fixed him with a glare, the words I have not just on the tip of my tongue. His blue eyes squeezed shut as he chuckled. "But I mean, so have I. I guess."

"Are you trying to tell me something, Lee?" My eyebrows raised, my eyes staring at him with a pleading gaze that clearly asked him to save this conversation for another time. Maybe when we're both married and have kids. Completely tied down where there can be no possibilities. "Cause you know that I don't want to hear it."

"You can chill, Jake. I'm not about to profess my love for you." He laughed in a way that sounded forced. All sorts of thoughts then broke out from the little box I kept locked away; thoughts that included what if's and maybe's. I shook my head inwardly and the box shut away again. I concentrated on acting unfazed.

"At least until," he began, his body rolling onto it's side which closed the distance between us. "You've figured out how you feel about me." I swallowed against the tightness in my throat, my eyes blinking excessively. Lee licked his lips in a slow manner that could only be suggestive. My breathing took a dip in the shallow end as my heart beat accelerated.

"You know what we've never done, Jake?" I shook my head from left to right, in place of vocally saying no. He smiled briefly, his eyes dropping lower before flitting back to my eyes. "Kissed." His voice was barely above a whisper. "We've never kissed, Jake." My mouth opened slightly to allow short, silent breaths out; feeble way to calm myself down but I did it anyway. Lee shuffled closer, to get anymore closer seemed impossible.

I wanted to look away, but I didn't dare; I needed to watch his every move, I needed to know what he was going to do. I should leave, I thought, but I didn't listen. His hand rested lightly against my cheek, the pad of his thumb brushing over the skin beneath my eye before moving lower to slide across my bottom lip. My breathing was ragged now, I didn't dare speak. Lee's eyes kept flickering from my lips to my eyes, assessing my actions and looking for the moment where I made it clear I didn't want him to. He seemed to think of my lack of control over my rationality as an invitation.

His face inched closer to mine to the point where I could feel his breath burn against my lips. His tongue peeked from behind his top lip, sliding over his teeth. A small hint of a smile hovering just above the surface. My chest rushed with something similar to excitement, following through into my stomach where it stayed, swirling. Lee's hand curled around the back of my neck, his fingers sliding into my hair and tightening as he pulled my head forward. Our foreheads tilting to meet and our eyes unsure of where to focus; jumping from lips to eyes.

My eyes fluttered against the heat my face seemed to be emanating now, my hands balled into fists at my side. Lee tilted his head upward in one swift motion, our lips connecting in a soft, slow, closed-mouthed kiss. My eyes opened as Lee leaned back cautiously, looking for my reaction. It took me a moment, my head felt jumbled and everything seemed upside down. My bottom lip was still wet from Lee's kiss and it took me a moment to realise that I'd just flicked my tongue out to run over them.

That's when reality slammed into me hard. My body flew up in a rush and I launched myself from the bed. The main thought circling my mind was the fact that I'd got my best friends saliva stirring around inside me. I had a sudden urge to spit but I kept myself under control. Lee was now sitting upright on the edge of his bed, looking up at me with a panicked expression.

"Wha- what did you do," it wasn't a question that left my voice in a high pitched murmur, but more of a realisation. "Lee, what the fuck?" My voice was straining to keep itself low, shock the more prominent emotion at that moment. My breathing was faster than before now, my head pounding with words that told me I wanted it and words that told me to smack him. I paced back and forth, trying not to think about what'd just happened, which wasn't successful since the most dominant thought was of Lee's fucking lips.

"I can't do this," I muttered, storming my way over to the door.

"Wait, Jake, please just wait," I stopped, but I didn't turn around to face him. Problem was, I didn't need to, because Lee did that for me. His hand took a firm grip on my arm and twirled me around, my feet stumbling backwards so my back pressed up against the door. "Don't leave," Lee's eyes looked up at me through his lashes - a heavy feeling of regret emanated from them. His other hand came to rest by my shoulder on the door, bracing his body. His eyes were flicking all over my face, as if he was trying to find the words to tell me to just stay, to not leave.

"I'm sorry," he whispered. "I thought you- you didn't back away, Jake. I just thought-"

"Well you thought wrong, Lee," I forced anger into my features, with a look that asked him to back away. He decided to completely ignore it and step a little closer. I would've moved back, if it weren't for the fact that I was sandwiched between him and his bedroom door.

"You always do this." He said, his head dropping and shaking from side to side like a disappointed father. Reminded me all to much of my dad.

"Always do what?"

"This!" The hand that was gripping my arm moved to gesture between the two of us. "You lead me on, pretend you want it and act like it's just a game and then when I do something that doesn't suit you, you flip out!"

"You went beyond the game, Lee. You fucking kissed me." I gritted out, my jaw clenched. Lee huffed out a disbelieving laugh.

"Don't even fucking act like you didn't enjoy it," his eyes turned cold and his voice dropped low and dangerous. "That's why you lash out, isn't it? Because you hate that fact that you actually liked it." His lips quirked into a daring smirk. "You want me, don't you? You just don't want to admit it." Then, like the flick of a switch, his features grew soft and his eyes melted back to worry as he sighed. "Jake, please, just stay."

"No." I shoved him away and took the opportunity to quickly slip out of his room and out the front door. I stood there for a while, in the cold. The sky was just growing dark, merging into night. I started walking down the road, anywhere away from Lee's house where he couldn't find me. Once out of view, I reached into my pocket and pulled out my mobile which followed by deftly dialling the areas taxi firm.

The entire journey home was full of agonising replays of what'd just happened. But instead of them ending where they did, they continued into what might have happened if I'd leaned back in and kissed him again instead of jumping off the bed; my train of thought consisted of only Lee Towson, even after I'd reached my house and climbed into bed.

It used to be all fun and games, just me and Lee messing around and nobody needed to know. But kissing? Kissing changed things. I mean, come on; I never used to get a hard-on for him, and now I'm getting excited just by the mere memory of his lips touching mine? That's just... just wrong.

What the fuck am I going to do about school tomorrow? I can't just go back to how we were, I won't even be able to look at him without thinking about it. The worst thing about this is the fact that everyone just expects me and Lee to be glued to each other because that's how we've always been. I show up tomorrow and I act even the slightest bit different, one of them's going to notice something. I pulled the duvet over my head and stared into the darkness for a while before finally thinking: fuck it, and going to sleep.

Chapter 3

W hen I woke up this morning, it took my memory a while to remember what had happened last night. But it wasn't until I was passing the school gates that the anxiety fully hit me. My feet stopped in their tracks and my eyes skimmed across the familiar faces of my friends that were scattered between the main entrance doors and the gates, amongst many faces I'd never noticed before.

I licked my lips nervously and mentally shook my head, looking down at my feet I told myself to just simply put one foot in front of the other. I couldn't shake the feeling of everyone's eyes focused on me, but when I looked up it was as if I wasn't even there.

I let out the deep breath I'd been holding and quickly weaved my way into the building and the less-populated halls. I spared a quick sigh of relief before making my way over to my locker and sorting through what I needed and when. I thought I'd at least escaped confrontation with Lee for the better part of this morning, turns out I was wrong as I heard his familiar smooth, even voice from over my shoulder.

"Jake, can we talk?" I spun around to face him, my eyes skittered over the surrounding people that plagued the hall with their loud banter; anything to keep me from having to look into his eyes. I couldn't handle that right now. He repeated my name before tilting his head in a way of asking me to follow him. Unwanting to cause a scene, I obliged.

He took me down into the near-empty Maths corridors, just underneath the staircase that lead up to the R.E rooms. The quiet was unnerving. I propped my leg up against the wall I was leaning against, my eyes still avoiding contact with his knowing blue irises.

"Could you at least look at me?" His tone hinted that he thought I was being immature and pathetic, which just made me want to ignore him all the more. "Seriously?" I sighed and rolled my eyes. "Fine," he took a step towards me, the insides of my body jumped in alarm but I kept myself rigid to appear unaffected by his predatory gaze. My throat bobbed as I swallowed, my face growing hot and my palms clammy. I subtly wiped them against my jeans whilst clearing my throat.

"Does it really have to change things this much, Jake? It was a dumb kiss by a miscalculated judgement. My bad for wanting to dive into the deep end and take things a little further."

"Shut the fuck up, Lee, keep your voice down." My eyes jumped in line with his on impulse, panic a whirring noise inside my stomach at the loudness of his voice.

"I shouldn't have assumed, yeah, and I get that. But I think you're blowing things way out of proportion, dude." His voice didn't get any lower, which caused me to give him a sharp shush accompanied by pressing my index finger to my lips. He rolled his eyes. "Mate, I'm trying to apologise here, yeah, and all you can think about is who's listening. No one's even here, chill out and stop being so paranoid."

"Look, can we just not do this during school?"

"Like you'd give me the time of day anywhere else," he scoffed, taking another step forward. I had to agree with him there. His white sneakers shuffled towards me even more, only a small gap was left between us and I was beginning to feel nervous. My eyes darted from his shoes to his face, unsure of which part of his body I should really be focusing on. They definitely shouldn't have been focusing on that area they kept slyly skimming past, just below his belt, as they made their way up and down his person.

"You keep acting like this with me, someone's going to notice and wanna' know why. You do realise that, don't you?" I nodded in answer, watching him gingerly. "So either we just forget it ever happened and go back to normal, or we do something about it..." He trailed off, his eyes sliding to the left sheepishly. His feet closed the distance between us before I could move. His hands pressing against the wall either side of my head as he leaned in. The strong smell of our colognes mingling together.

My head was pushed up against the wall from the pressure of Lee's hand, his thumb underneath my chin tilting it upwards with his fingers resting against my cheek. My arms hung loosely by my sides, my brain not functioning properly enough to order them to shove him away. Apparently the lower part of my body disagreed with my head as my hips pushed forward, up against Lee's leg that was in between the two of mine. I managed to swallow back the moan that threatened to escape, thankfully.

"Lee, don't," I forced out, shaking my head from side to side half-heartedly. My eyes half-lidded, betraying my words along with the hoarseness of my voice. A devious smile curved Lee's lips up, making his eyes look dark as they took in every little detail of my mouth. "Lee," I insisted firmly, but the rest of my body made no efforts to push him away.

"Ehem..." I jumped in surprise from the sound of someone clearing their throat, I couldn't see who due to the fact that Lee was pressed up against me and holding my face directly towards his. Lee's eyes grew wide but a smile stayed evident on his lips before he took a step back and let his hand fall from it's grip on my face. His body half-turned to the side, which allowed me to see who'd interrupted us from our compromising position.

"You guys having another domestic?" Chase chuckled, completely oblivious to the sexual aspect our conversation had before he'd interrupted. Me and Lee nervously chuckled along with him in false agreement.

"Yeah, I was just telling Jake, here, that being a little bitch about things gets you no where." Lee smiled smugly that hid a meaning beneath it that Chase didn't understand, but, of course, I did. I fought the urge to stand on his foot and, or, kick him in the balls. The latter would have been more satisfying to watch, no doubt.

"Aah, what've you done to upset him now, Felix?" Chase mocked, putting on a stern expression. If he placed his hands on his hips, fixed a pout on his lips and did that mhm noise, it'd be like looking at my mother - granted she'd have an almost-shaved head, a darker skin colour and be wearing baggy jeans hanging off her arse...I cringed at that thought.

"Told him I wanna fuck" - my brain literally malfunctioned as soon as these words left Lee's mouth, my head was screaming 'shit, Jake run! The secret's out!' whilst my dick was thinking 'I like the sound of that'. It was all I could do to suppress the sigh as I heard the rest of Lee's sentence - "His sister." Before my face scrunched up in a sort of half-disgust, half-confused sort of way.

"Jake doesn't have a sister," Chase pointed out rather dumbly.

"That's part of the joke, CJ." Lee rolled his eyes and rested them upon me with a smirk, before he shot me a sly wink. I chose to ignore him and focused my attention towards Chase, who was standing there with his mouth in an 'O' shape as he caught on.

"Anyway, you guys wanna' head on up to the sixth form's common room? The guys are all waiting for us up there." Chase said, already turning to leave but stopping as he realised we weren't following him.

"Yeah, CJ, we'll meet you up there; you go ahead." Lee gestured with a nod of his head for him to continue on without us. As soon as Chase was out of sight, I smacked Lee around the head with my hand.

"Ouch-"

"What the fuck, Lee? You sodding wanker!" I screamed at him in a whisper.

"What?" He questioned incredulously, his pitch higher than usu-al.

"Told him I wanted to fuck his sister" - my tone was snide as I mimicked Lee's words in a petty way - "Seriously, man, what the fuck? What the fuck?" I stressed, but Lee just laughed.

"I thought it was funny. Should have seen your face when I said the word fuck," he continued to laugh, not paying me any attention as he lost himself in his own humour. I fought the urge to smack him again, and walked ahead to the common room. When I arrived there, I spotted my usual group hanging out at the usual far corner of the room, by the Foosball table.

"Ey up Lads," I greeted with an over-confident grin. I was welcomed how I normally always am, lots of bro-hugs and slaps on the back, couple of cheers tossed in there as well, for no particular reason. I glanced down at the foosball table where Tyler, the shortest lad of our group, and Owen, the football-obsessed scottish man, were currently involved in a game. "Who's winning, then?"

"Me, obviously, 'cause am bloody damn good." Owen boasted, shooting me a side-ways grin. I returned it with a quirk of an eyebrow. Smiling, I leaned against the wall, out of the way of my crowd of friends surrounding Tyler and Owen. I was joined not soon after by Lee, unsurprisingly. It's funny how one little thing can make someone go from enjoying their mates company to wishing they would just sod off.

Lee propped one leg up against the wall, standing next to me and leaning into my shoulder slightly. He turned his head so his lips were centimetres from touching my ear, and whispered, "Do you reckon I could make you come just with words?" I didn't need to see his face to know that he was smirking. "It'd be sort of kinky, wouldn't it? To do it right now, in front of everyone. To make you come in your pants."

"Lee," I warned in a deep tone, keeping my voice low and my eyes on the lads in front. I felt something brushing down the side of my thigh, gently and barely there, but I didn't want to lift my gaze from watching out for unwanted eyes that might get the wrong idea - or the right idea - about what Lee was doing. The gentle brush moved further up my thigh and across, towards my zipper, becoming less gentle and more provocative.

"I bet you I could. Right here." His hot breath breezed against my ear and down my neck as he spoke, his voice barely above a whisper. "You keep shaking your head, Jake, just makes you look all the more eager for it." If it was even possible, I'd say his voice dropped even lower and more seductive; the length in my pants was beginning to twitch with arousal and my breathing grew shallow.

I could feel his fingers fiddling with the zip on my jeans, like he was playing with me about whether he would or wouldn't pull it down. I was hoping to God he wouldn't. And I was hoping to God that he'd just shut the fuck up, too. Strangely enough, his words stopped but that was the cause of his lips enclosing around my ear lobe licking the edge with his tongue and sucking, his teeth gently nipping at my skin.

I swallowed, finding it hard to keep my concentration on the other people. I was screwed if someone saw, but I just couldn't move. My attention was drifting and my dick was hardening and I was just fucking losing control.

And Lee was bloody smirking.

His hand withdrew from my zipper and I looked at him warily. "Fuckin' slut," he muttered, his smirk widening to a grin. I took a deep breath and chewed the inside of my cheek to calm myself down.

"You're such a dick, Lee."

Chapter 4

"I told you, she was just a work colleague," Lee's father's voice bellowed from the lounge. I sat on the third step from the bottom as I looked down at where Lee was sitting, right on the last step. His forehead resting against the banister stand, his blonde hair dishevelled from the earlier occurrence it had with his hands - when he'd ran them through his locks obsessively from frustration.

It was dark, the light emanating from the doorway, where his dad and mum were conversing, was the only thing keeping us from sitting in darkness.

My chest felt heavy as I recalled what Lee had told me when he rang me up about an hour ago. I wasn't talking to him, for obvious reasons, but with the way his voice was shaking - straining to even push out the few words he managed to speak - I couldn't ignore him. I couldn't neglect the responsibilities of being a best friend, my conscience wouldn't let me.

I raced straight over, finding him in his bedroom where he was sat hugging his knees. He won't admit when he looks back at it, but there were visible streaks of tears running down his cheeks as he'd explained to me that he'd caught his dad with another woman. Well, he was doing a lot more than just being with the woman, from what I heard. Lee had told his mother, and when his dad returned home, that's when we found ourselves on the steps, listening in on the confrontation.

"Alexandra, you know I would never do such a disgus-"

"And all the late nights at the office, Tony, were you with her?" Lee's mum's voice cut his dad's off, their argument droning in the distance. I was thankful that Kimberly and the other Towson son, Murphy, wasn't around to hear it. But it killed me that Lee was, out of all of them, Lee was the one that'd always hoped to continue having a happy family. I didn't want him to listen to it, asked him to go on a walk with me, but he refused.

I slid down the steps separating me and Lee, stopping by his side where I wrapped an arm around his shoulder. With his head hung low, he fell against me and I wrapped my arm around him tighter before sliding it into his hair and resting my cheek atop his head. His body shivered from the heavy breaths he was taking, trying to force the tears away - because he'd be damned if he'd let himself be weak, as he put it.

"Come on," I whispered. "Let's go." I didn't give him a choice, grabbing his wrist in my grip and pulling him up. He barely seemed to have the strength or determination to stand, his body slouching against mine. I pulled him towards the door and, very quietly, opened and shut it behind us. The air was cold and dark with only a slight breeze to tinge our cheeks a pale red.

I could hear him sniffling into his sleeve as I walked us both, clumsily, down to the river that we liked to think of our place. It was only a short walk away, down through a muddy field, we arrived at the small, grassy bridge that arched over a stream. The noise of the water flowing underneath us was calming. I perched him against the bridges' wall where I sat myself beside him and waited patiently until he felt like talking. I didn't have to wait long.

"I don't get it, Jake," he began, wiping the tears away. "This wasn't supposed to happen."

"I know Lee," he abruptly stood up, turning on me with a pure look of anger.

"No, you don't fucking know! You're fine, Jake, your parents are still fucking together!" He yelled, his face turning red and the veins on his forehead standing out. "How could you possibly know what it's like?" He said through gritted teeth. I didn't react the way he wanted, he was just cruising for a fight that I wasn't about to give him. He soon realised and decided to stick with talking.

"Just- just seeing him with that...whore... just fucking made me sick." His face demonstrated his feelings before he broke out in a surge of frustration and kicked his foot, hard, against the brick wall of the bridge. I made a wise decision in staying silent. "I can't believe he would do this. Everything was great, just fucking awesome, and he had to go screw it up." He started up kicking the wall again and I had the urge to stop him, but I thought it was best to just let him work his anger out of his system.

But kicking soon turned to punching; the ridged, sharp edges of the bricks cutting against the skin of his fists with every hit. I wasn't listening to the incoherent bursts of insults and curses aimed towards his father's name as I grabbed either side of his arms and pushed him back, up against the other side of the bridge wall; pinning him there, struggling against the shoves as he fought to calm down.

"Lee, just fucking chill," my voice was loud and echoing across the area of fields that surrounded us. "It's okay, just calm down. You're bleeding." He continued to ignore me. "Stop!" I resorted to shouting, shoving him harder against the wall, painfully. He ceased struggling and just stood there, his chest rising and falling heavily whilst he huffed out breaths of air that wisped off in swirls of grey mist.

I dropped my hands to his wrists and raised them between us, examining the damage that was barely visible in the dim light, from the single street lamp that loomed over us by our side. The cuts were shallow but his knuckles were beaten up pretty bad. He's always had a bit of an anger problem.

"Look at you, you're a fuckin' mess Lee."

"Thanks," he muttered, his voice so low I hardly heard it. My eyes flickered up to connect with his, we held gazes in silence for a few moments. "Jake, please," he whispered, choking back the tears. It was vague, but I knew what he meant, and my heart mentally sunk in my chest.

"I can't, Lee." I dropped my eyes down to our hands, my fingers wrapped around his wrists to avoid staining them with the blood that dripped from Lee's. I swallowed and chewed the inside of my cheek.

"Why not?" I briefly wished he'd raise his voice a little so I could hear him better, but also wished I couldn't hear him at all.

"Because I don't--I can't-- I'm not into you like that." I kept my head low, not willing to see his expression and hoping he wouldn't kick off like the time bomb he is. Each day I'm just waiting for him to explode; he's so unpredictable it's scary.

"Yeah...don't give me that bullshit, Jake. It's fucking obvious you got somethin' hot for me." Suddenly, his tone took a u-turn from sad to humorous.

"What the fuck? How'd you come to that conclusion?"

"It's written all over your face when you look at me, mate, and I'm not even gonna' start on what's going on in your pants..." A blush crawled it's way up my cheeks, in spite of my defense. I turned my head to the side, away from the light. Lee's hand left my grip and his thumb and forefinger tilted my chin back to meet his gaze. "Why are you so stubborn?" I chose not to grace that question with an answer.

"Look, if you're feeling better I'm gonna' head on home." I stepped back and made to leave before Lee took a hold on my arm and pulled me back to face him.

"Seriously? Just gonna' ditch when things approach a subject you're too much of a dick to deal with?"

"I don't wanna' talk about it right now, okay?" I glanced down at his hand still wrapped around my arm, the blood thankfully dried and not currently staining my white jacket.

"You never wanna' talk about it, Jake." His tone was bored, his eyes rolled and he sighed, pulling me closer. His gaze alternated between staring into my eyes or at my lips - occasionally they'd look up at my hair.

"Yeah, well maybe there's a reason for that-"

"So what's the reason?" He interjected eagerly, anticipating the answer with excitement. I closed my eyes and took a deep breath.

"Let go of me, Lee." I murmured. I heard him chuckle quietly, but he did the opposite and tugged me closer.

"Tell me first." I could feel his eyes burning expectantly against my face. That urge began welling up inside me, and before I could weigh out the pros and cons and what was right and what wasn't, I surged forward. My lips slammed against Lee's, our teeth clashing together with a brief shoot of pain. His feet stumbled backwards from the impact and, probably, a little out of shock.

I pulled his bottom lip into my mouth with my teeth, sucking. A small sound of a moan came from Lee's mouth as I did so. His grip on my arm released and his hand fisted into my hair, with his other finding a place against my hip. A rhythm developed and our lips moved in time, my head being pulled to the side so Lee could deepen the kiss. He wasn't one for holding back, apparently.

The hand on my hip slid it's way under my shirt. My back curved inward, away from the freezing touch of his fingers but wanting more all the same. I shoved him backwards, against the wall of the bridge again, our lips not once losing contact; our mouths complementing each other with appreciative gasps and slight moans. I hooked both my thumbs in the belt loops of his jeans, pulling his hips forward to increase the friction.

"Fuck, Jake," he managed to mutter. I found myself kissing along his jaw line, a hand sliding into his hair to pull his head to the side, gaining better access to his neck. My teeth nipping at the taut skin before sucking and licking. "Oh, God, shit,"

I paused to whisper against his neck, "You're very articulate tonight," with a hint of a smile playing around on my otherwise occupied lips.

"Sod off." Was his reply. I pulled back to laugh, unable to hold it in.

Chapter 5

I sat on the sofa watching the music channel, waiting for my parents to eventually leave the house so I could have it all to myself. It's a Thursday and, according to mum, Thursdays are date days. Yes, my parents still go on dates even though they've been married for fifteen years. Romantic, isn't it? I inwardly rolled my eyes. I could distantly hear the click of my mothers heels before she appeared, sauntering through the doorway of the living room in a sleek deep-purple dress.

"Jake, darling, Amanda made you dinner for tonight, if you get hungry. We won't be back till late so don't forget to lock up before you go to bed." She gave me a gentle smile that meant absolutely nothing, and shouted for dad. He came into view not a few moments later wearing his usual black tie suit.

"Okay, we'll be going." He turned his gaze towards me with that not-so-warm glare of his and said, "Behave."

"Since when do I ever not?" I retorted. He raised his eyebrows and I could see that he was mentally straining to hold back a full on rant.

He ushered mum towards the door, and just before he left he turned back as he remembered something.

"The maid's check for last week is on the kitchen side, don't forget to pay her before she leaves." I nodded in acknowledgement, returning my attention to the television. They exited the house and I sighed in relief. Good riddance. With a huff and a quick stretch, I pushed myself to my feet and made my way through the hall to the kitchen where I found Amanda.

"Hey Mandy, what's up?" I leaned against the opposite side of the counter to where she was standing. Her blonde hair gathered up in a bun on top of her head, showing off her naturally tanned skin. Feels like I haven't seen her in years, she's changed so much from when she first started, when she was twenty-two. She's now somewhere around thirty.

"Jake, it's good to see you around here. Ever since you've grown into a young man you seem to have just been swept of the face of the earth." She laughed quietly; a smile that genuinely made you feel good. She's been our maid since I was about three.

"Yeah..." I contemplated whether to talk to her about my current situation with Lee or not. I've felt like I could tell her everything my whole life but, I don't know, this topic seems a bit too personal. Not that she'd care, she's more of a mother than my actual mum. I decided to touch on the subject, only slightly. "Lee's parents are going through a rough time," Amanda looked up from where she was wiping down the marble counter top.

"Oh?" She was too polite to ask what I meant, but I knew she desperately wanted to find out. Just the tone of her voice let it on.

"Yeah. His dad, Tony, went and cheated with someone at the office. Lee was gutted, but I haven't spoken to him for three days since it happened."

"Oh that's a shame. They always seemed so happy..." She muttered into space. Her voice grew louder as she refocused on her cleaning whilst slyly sneaking peeks up at me. I fought to keep my brows from furrowing in suspicion. "You know, I haven't seen Felix in a while, you never bring him over anymore."

Cautiously, I replied. "Things have been a little...weird with us at the moment." Her head instantly shot up, silently demanding more information. I shook my head and dropped my gaze yet again. "It's nothing, really." She pouted her lips in thought, trying to keep a smile at bay whilst she watched my face like she was evaluating me. Thankfully at this moment, behind the kitchen blinds, a bright light beamed through against the darkness of the night sky. I could hear the unmistakable sound of tires tearing up the gravel of our drive.

Amanda didn't waste no time in bustling off to answer the door after the sound of the bell echoed inside the house. I waited in the kitchen patiently, until Amanda shouted, "Jake, you have a visitor!" With which I lazily dragged my feet to the double doors that were the entrance to my house. Approaching the open door that Mandy was still standing at, I peeked around to see, first, at her feet a black duffel bag. I didn't need to see his face, I've seen that duffel many times before to know who it belonged to.

Mandy turned to face me with a wide grin before muttering, "Look Jake, it's raining outside. Invite the poor boy in!" Before giving me a cheeky wink and disappearing from my sight. I looked out behind Felix to find that it wasn't actually raining, but just for reassurance I listened intensely.

"It's not actually raining, Jake." Instead of the sound of pattering rain, I was greeted with Lee's monotone voice. I slowly nodded, feeling only slightly like an idiot, as I stepped aside and gestured for Lee to come in. He took the offer with no hesitation. After taking more time than really needed to shut the door, I graced Lee with an awkward look of welcome. He glanced down at his bag before peering up at me shyly. "So, uh, I was sort of hoping I could stay here for a while?"

"Something happened?"

"My 'rents are doing my head in. They're constantly arguing, which sent Kimberly packing off to her mates and Murphy to a hotel. I was the last one and decided not to stick around." He shrugged, adding, "Well, I mean, if it's okay to stay here..." I pretended to contemplate it, holding him in suspense.

"Sure, of course." My eyes, for some reason, wouldn't quit staring down at my feet as we spoke. I jerked my head in the direction of the lounge and then followed on to lead him through. He trailed behind me silently. "So...do you want to put that upstairs?" I pointed towards his bag.

"Yeah, probably be a good idea." His smile made me feel uncomfortable.

"Okay, well you know where the guest room is." I quirked one corner of my lip up as if I was smiling to a complete stranger. I wanted to slap myself for acting so strange. Lee half-turned to leave but stopped and twisted back to face me.

"Yeah, could you show me again? My head is just...pfft...gone at the moment." He chuckled, heaving his bag over his shoulder and waiting for me to lead the way. I wanted to avoid going anywhere alone with the guy, but clearly that wasn't on his agenda tonight. I set off towards the stairs, taking them two at a time and coming to a stop as I reached the top. When you're upstairs, it feels completely separate from the bottom half of the house. Almost Secluded.

Lee moved past me and down the left side of the hall, straight to the bottom, where inside the last door resided my bedroom. I stared in wonder for a moment before chasing after him. My door was left open and Lee had set his duffel on top of my double bed but he wasn't anywhere in sight. I nervously peered around my door frame into the rest of my room, but in seeing no glimpse of him I came to the conclusion that he was hiding in the en-suite.

"Lee? You do realise this isn't the guest room, right?" I called, stepping cautiously into the room, my eyes locked on the closed door to my bathroom.

"Yeah, I know." His voice came from behind me, all smooth and dark and devious. I turned on my heels to see him pushing the door to my bedroom shut with a soft thud. I swallowed as he took a step forward. "You've been avoiding me,"

"Have I?" My voice cracked into a high pitched squeak as I spoke, a burn of embarrassment darkening my cheeks a deep red. He took a few more steps.

"Mhm. After our little scene on the bridge you just went M.I.A,"

I cleared my throat in order to force out, "Really? I hadn't noticed." I blinked excessively when his right hand slid it's way up my torso to rest against the back of my neck. He leaned his forehead against mine, peering up at me through his lashes. His blue eyes seeming brighter than ever at such a close distance.

"I have," he whispered. "I was a little confused. It's not like we left that night on a bad note..." His voice was low and sad.

"I just needed a bit of time to-"

"So you admit it?" He cut me off, pulling his head back - even if only slightly.

"Admit what?" My eyebrows furrowed and my feet desperately wanted to take a step back. But taking a step back meant that I'd be moving closer to the bed, and that was something I really needed to avoid.

"That you've been distant." He replied. "So how've you been?" My head shook on it's own accord, my mind trying to keep up with the fast changing conversation. I could feel his other hand pushing against my chest, urging me to walk backwards. I ignored it, hoping he'd give up.

"Uh, oh-okay, I guess?" I stammered, not knowing what to expect from him. The hand on my chest pushed more firmly, his feet stepping forward in a way that forced me to take a step back.

"Good to hear. I'm great, too, by the way. I talked to your girlfriend the other day," I couldn't keep my eyes to stay still as they flickered from his left eye to his right. It wasn't the fact that he was so close that was unnerving me, but the fact that he seemed to just be making idle chit-chat. And then his teeth sunk down on his bottom lip and it was like my eyes instantly knew where to look right at the wrong time. I swallowed back the gasp, choking only a little.

The hand curled around my neck slid down to the collar of my shirt, where it was joined by the other and, together, began undoing the buttons of my shirt. "She told me she hadn't seen you for two weeks. Wait- wasn't that right about the time that we first started getting hard for each other, Jake? Bit of a coincidence, hey?" He huffed out an emotionless laugh, his eyes engulfed by hunger.

His fingers paused half way down my shirt and, unexpectedly, shoved me back so my feet stumbled until my knees hit the edge of my bed and I had no choice but to fall back into the mattress. My mouth hung open, little gasps of air escaping in rushed breaths. I was inhaling and exhaling at an unnatural speed.

He loomed over me intimidatingly, his eyes raking over my body and stopping at the buckle of my belt - at least I hoped he was staring at the buckle. Before I could even register what was happening, his fingers were slipping the button of my jeans open and sliding the zipper down. Eventually I kicked my body into action, pushing my torso up and grabbing his wrists in a silent way of telling him to stop.

But he just smiled, wrenching his arms free and, in return, fixing a tight grip on my own wrists. He pushed the top half of my body back onto the bed and straddled my chest, pinning my hands either side of my head. That damn mischievous smirk curled his lips up at the edges, his teeth nipping at the inside of his bottom lip.

"I'm having a sense of deja vú, Jake. Except now I'm on top." He stated with a voice that sent my blood rushing in the completely wrong direction.

Chapter 6

I swallowed against the tightness in my throat that was slowly intensifying. My eyes fluttering as they stared up at Lee's face, his mouth playing with a smirk, a mischievous glint in his eyes. My whole body was overwhelmed by heat, and I was trying to decide - as a distraction for myself - if Amanda had turned the heating up, or if I was having a hot flush. None of them seemed likely, if I was honest with myself. At that moment, Lee pushed more pressure onto my wrist that were pinned to the mattress by his knees.

My eyes shot to his. "Why've you been avoiding me?" He asked me, his voice low but with an undertone of hurt. The words I haven't were on the tip of my tongue, but I couldn't say it because I didn't want to lie. Truth is, I was a little disgusted with myself for lusting after my best friend. Male best friend. I know that if my parents ever found out, they'd disown me. It would be a disgrace to their family name. But at the moment, looking up at him, I couldn't give a shit.

"I think you know the reason why, Lee." I muttered, but I know he still heard it by the shift of his weight as he leaned back. The smirk was wiped from his lips and his knees released my wrists. His eyes looked down on me, not even bothering to hide his disappointment.

"Seriously? Turning homophobic on me now, Jake?" I furrowed my brows and propped myself up on my elbows.

"What? No, of course not. That's not what I meant," I paused, taking a breath and scanning my eyes through the air like I was searching for the words, as if they were hiding from me. "Look, it's just really new to me and I had to get my head around it."

"How the fuck is it new to you? We've been messing around since we were fourteen!" He practically screamed and my hand instantly shot up to slap him before a sharp shush left my lips. He looked at me with bewilderment.

"Mandy's still here, I really don't need her knowing about this." I whispered with irritation. He rolled his eyes in return. I fidgeted underneath his body that was still weighing down my chest. "Can you get off me now?"

"No." Was his snappy answer. I sighed and collapsed back down into the duvets, a slight ache around my elbows and shoulders as they were released from the strain of holding my torso up. I could feel his stare burning against my skin expectantly, waiting for me to continue.

"When we used to fool around, that's all it was; we just messed with each other. We never meant anything by it, didn't feel anything for each other-"

"So you feel something for me?" Lee interrupted, that smirk fixed back in it's place. I fought the itch to smack it off.

"Yes. No. I...don't know. Maybe?" My pitch grew higher at the last word, gazing up at him with confusion at my own answer. He didn't seem like he was about to add his own opinion in, so I carried on. "I guess now that we're older, it's just different. We're more..."

"Horny?"

"No."

"Sexual?"

"No! Lee just shut up and let me speak." He stayed silent, so I took that as my que. "We're more..." I couldn't find a sensible way to explain it, so I just gave up. "Oh fuck it. Yes, we're more horny." Lee smiled with victory. I rolled my eyes to the side and decided to concentrate on my chest of drawers.

It was only a few seconds later that Lee stood up, his trainers leaving dirt marks on my duvet, and jumped down from the bed. My eyes flickered up to the full length mirror that was positioned to the left of my drawers, waiting for him to come into view.

At first, I could only see half of his body; moving in and out of view whilst I heard him fiddling with the zipper on his duffel. I wondered what he was doing but didn't remove my eyes from the mirror. A few piles of clothes came into view, landing on top of my bed as he tossed them out - I briefly wondered how long he'd expected to stay here for - then the rest of his body came into view as he moved to the side, his hand ruffling up his fringe before instantly - like he just knew - flicking his eyes up to mine at the mirror. I flinched at the intensity of his gaze, but didn't look away.

His fingers played with his shirt at the bottom, before sliding his hands beneath the material, slowly and almost painfully, before pulling it deftly over his head. My gaze slid unwillingly over his defined abs before flashing back to his stare. My stomach swirled as if hot liquid was slipping it's way south through my body. My breathing quickened but I managed to keep that unnoticeable. The flush that stained my cheeks, however, was a different story.

Lee's face was emotionless, empty. His hands dropping down to the button on his jeans, quickly and efficiently undoing it and wasting no time in sliding the zipper down too. I didn't know what to expect, and I wanted to leave but I felt glued to my place. My eyes resting at the top of his - now viewable - black boxers. He let his jeans fall to the floor before clearing his throat in a cocky, arrogant manner. My eyes lurched towards his, finding one of his golden eyebrows raised and a smug smile set on his lips.

"Don't mind if I take a shower, do you?" He said, his voice composed but plagued by amusement at the same time. I suddenly just wanted to face palm from embarrassment, but settled for shutting my eyes. I heard him chuckle before hearing the en-suite door close and lock. When I opened my eyes again, the pile of clothes on my bed was gone. I huffed out a large breath of air that I was holding in and pushed myself from my bed.

With a moments hesitation, I closed my bedroom door behind me and jogged back down the stairs only to collapse on the couch, my forearm resting across my eyes. I could distantly hear Amanda humming to a tune from the kitchen. I should probably go get her check and let her off for the night, but that would mean being completely alone with Lee for at least five hours. Depending on my parents even making it home instead of stopping at a hotel, like usual. But hey, I got no complaints for them doing their business somewhere far, far from where I am.

Thankfully, though, I didn't have to move because Amanda came sauntering in whilst whistling a very familiar tune. She smiled sweetly at me as I sat up, nodding my head towards her in acknowledgement. She gave me a sympathetic look before perching on the sofa next to me. I cocked one eyebrow and was about to ask her why she was looking at me like that, but she beat me to the first word.

"Where's Felix?" The stare she fixed me with made me feel like she knew. It was one of those awkward moments where you tug on your collar to loosen it. But I kept my hands entwined and resting on my knees.

"Taking a shower," I attempted to keep my voice casual, and to keep my thoughts from drifting to provocative images. I thought it was best to change the subject. "Dad said your check's on the kitchen side, by the way. Don't forget it before you leave." She nodded her head gently.

"Ah, tell your father I said thank you." She grinned. I slid my phone from my pocket and checked the time: nine-thirty.

"Shit, Mandy you've done thirty minutes over-time."

"Jake! Language!" She scolded, giving me a very stern expression. I rolled my eyes and contemplated arguing with the fact that I'm sixteen now, but decided against it. "And it's okay, I don't mind sticking around here a little longer than needed. It's not exactly hell." She winked with a smile. "But yes, my husband will be waiting for me so I best be off. You'll be okay, you and Felix?" I felt like saying no but kept my mouth shut and just nodded.

She returned the nod and disappeared towards the kitchen. I waited patiently for her to come back through, for some reason, wanting to be polite and wave her off. It only took a few minutes and I was at the front door, holding it open for her.

"Have fun, but keep safe." She dropped her chin and raised her eyebrows and I couldn't even believe what she was insinuating. But by the time I'd gotten over the shock, she was driving away.

What the fuck? was all I could think.

I slammed the door harder than necessary, turning back into the living room to find Lee with his arms crossed across his chest and his legs outstretched and crossed at the ankle. I shoved my hands in my pockets and shuffled forward, looking down at the beige carpet. I was expecting him to crack an innuendo or something, but he just sat there, waiting. That didn't particularly help my nerves.

"Are you going to sit down?" He asked me, nodding his head towards the space next to him on the white sofa. My gaze drifted to the single seater to my right but my legs directed me towards Lee. I fell into the sofa cushions carelessly, and we sat there in silence very awkwardly for a few moments. I glanced to the side to see Lee tapping his fingers in a fast beat on his knees before he said, "Wanna make out?"

"Sod off, Lee." I rubbed my forehead with my fingers, trying to work away the stress and embarrassment; the nervousness and the insecurities. I honestly don't know what's going on with me alately. I heard Lee laughing to the side of me, which just made me annoyed.

"What?" He chuckled. "I was only asking."

"I'm not in the mood." I groaned.

"For what, making out?"

"Lee, enough with the God damn- oh just shut the fuck up." I waved my hand in dismissal, suddenly feeling tired and letting a quick yawn escape.

"What the fuck's got you so up-tight?" I could just see his judgmental stare, just because he can't get his own bloody way. I couldn't be bothered to answer him, so I merely sighed, closing my eyes. I could feel his weight shifting on the other side of the sofa before he pratically threw himself into my lap, his knees either side of my hips.

I looked up at him with a look of warning, dropping my hands to my sides. But, like the dick he is, he just smiled.

"You know, you really need to chill." His palms slid up, over my chest, to rest on my shoulders. His fingers gently rubbing circles into my skin through the material of my shirt. My eyes slid shut without my consent. His fingers slowly increased in pressure and fuck did it feel good. His hands moved from my shoulders, up to my neck and continued with the same motions. I let my forehead fall forward and rest against Lee's chest. The pads of his fingers were warm and he really knew what he was doing. I bit my bottom lip and drew it into my mouth, sucking on it, to keep me from saying anything.

But my hands found Lee's wrists and pulled them down, my head lolling back and my eyes looking up at him lazily. I was about to tell him that I can't do it, it's too intimate. But he was leaning down and his eyes were focused on mine and then, in the split of a second, his lips were on mine and it wasn't my teeth, now, that were biting down on my bottom lip. His moans were causing vibrations, which just made his kiss that much more amazing. My brain was slowly losing rationality. All that I could process was: Lee, fuck, more, yes. And the only thing stopping me from saying it out loud was Lee's lips.

Chapter 7

Lee's hands were fisted in my hair now, pulling my head to the right for a better angle, desperately trying to deepen the kiss. His teeth scraping across my bottom lip every couple of seconds. His cotton-clad knees were digging into the sofa cushions, pushing his hips against my stomach, begging for friction. It got me hot just thinking that my best friend had a hard-on for me, but feeling it pressing against me was a whole new level of arousal.

I found my hands trailing down Lee's white tee, searching for the hem. All I could process - among the thoughts of how good Lee's mouth was - was getting rid of his top. Right now. My fingers eventually found the end and wasted no time in pinching it between them and tugging it over his head, leaving his blonde, wet, hair a tasseled mess. But God damn if he didn't look sexy. I stared at him in awe, admiring his more than perfect body.

I bit my bottom lip to hold back a gasp, peering up at Lee through my lashes with a burning look of want. I itched to say something, but all coherent thoughts flew out of my brain and I was left with scrambled words that made no sense. It was like being attacked by a thousand feelings and trying to name just one.

I think Lee mistook the delay in actions as a hesitation as he fumbled for words, coming out stuttered. "Jake- I- don't, I mean, we don't have to do this. I didn't mean to be forceful- was I forceful? Cause I swear I didn't mean to be..."

"Lee,"

"...It's just, fuck, you're so fucking sexy and it's like every time you look at me, you're just mind fucking me..."

"Lee," I tried again, this time with impatience.

"...I don't know dude, maybe I'm too pushy for you because I've already done this before and you haven't. Woah, shit! Fuck, that wasn't supposed to come out, fuck!" He burst into a world of curses, spitting them out like there was no tomorrow. His cheeks turned scarlet and his bright blue eyes were blown wide.

"Wow. Okay." I took a moment to run his words through my mind again. But I came to the decision that I'd deal with it another time, no more backing out and no more interruptions. I flipped him over to the side, onto his back, climbing on top of him with an excited smile. "We're definitely talking about that later, but right now we're gonna' fuck." I pointed my finger towards him, cocking an eyebrow at him to let him know that I wasn't going to forget it.

I shifted against his body, finding it a little uncomfortable trying to fit on the sofa with him. With a lick of the lips, I leaned in and placed a lingering kiss on his bottom lip, nipping at it gently before moving on to kiss down his jaw line. When I reached the crook of his neck, I paused momentarily to take in his scent and then focused on a particular spot, sucking at the skin and flicking out my tongue, catching the salty taste of Lee's body.

I slid my hands down his side, sliding my fingers underneath the waistband of his joggers and decided that it was about time we took this to the bedroom. Lee looked up at me with disappointment as I stood up, but smirked when I took his hand and pulled him up to follow me. He knew exactly where we were going, I didn't even have to say a word. He raced past me, climbing the stairs backwards and smirking down at me.

"Come on then, Jake, hurry up." He encouraged, turning on his heels and jogging the rest of the way. I sped up my pace, returning the smiles, and before I knew it I was slamming the door shut and stripping off my shirt.

You know that feeling of complete satisfaction after you release a whole load of built up tension? That's exactly what I was feeling as I lay on my back by Lee's side, the sheets of my bed tucked around our waists. I was still breathing quite deeply, one of my arms resting atop of my chest while the other was tucked behind my head. The only sound that could be heard was the inhale and exhale of air.

It'd been silent for quite a while, but after having sex with your best friend, what exactly do you say to break the ice? 'Nice fuck, wanna' go again?' I was still bloody recovering, there's no way I'm going another round in the same damn night. But then I remembered the little secret Lee had accidentally blurted out, and decided that it was a decent conversation starter.

"So about your little slip-up, when exactly did you start getting it off with lads?" Lee chuckled, most likely from embarrassment.

"I was kind of hoping you'd forgotten about that," he muttered before, "I've always known I was into guys, just never had the balls to go out and experiment. But the end of the last year at the 'School's out' party, I got wasted, and you know what I'm like when I'm on a high - absolutely fuckin' crazy." He paused in his explanation, like he was taking a moment to remember it all.

I turned my head to look at him as a prompt to tell me more. "Anyway, there was this guy who kept looking me up and down, so I took that as a hint and we took it to a room. At least, I think it was a room; we didn't exactly do it on a bed..." he trailed off, almost like he was ashamed. "Since then I just...didn't really care. I mean, I never hit on anyone at school, too risky. But people I know, know of a guy who got me a fake I.D and I hit the clubs." He gave me a sly wink, grinning.

"How come you never told me?"

"Guess I thought you'd freak out or something. Until I started noticing the way your stare lingered on my lips and...other areas." He turned his gaze back to the ceiling, that grin still fixed in place, looking more smug now, than anything. I rolled my eyes but couldn't keep the faint blush away. "Plus, the fact that you liked to mess around with me clearly indicated you weren't straight."

"Dude, I'm still straight. I'm like those rulers, you know, the flexible ones,"

"Oh, I know you're flexible," he said in a provocative tone, slipping me a quick wink before turning his head back. I fought the urge to elbow him, or jump on top of him - the latter sounded more fun.

"Shut up, Lee," I rolled my eyes, my cheeks growing hotter. But he just laughed in return. I sighed in content, letting the conversation fall into comfortable silence. But it didn't stay comfortable for long because I, being an idiot, completely forgot that my parent's were even still on earth. And so when I heard them slam the front door shut and shout out my name from the bottom of the stairs, my heart jumped up my throat and I fell off the edge of my bed with a heavy thud and a loud, "Fuck!"

I scrambled around for my clothes, tossing Lee his whilst I was at it. "Hurry up, get your clothes on. Quick!" I could hear my mother's voice calling out my name, accompanied by the sound of footsteps climbing the stairs. "Shit, shit, shit," I muttered as I threw on my shirt and pulled on my jeans. I briefly saw Lee shuffling towards the bathroom as he struggled with his joggers, trying to pull them up and run at the same time.

After watching Lee stumble through the en-suite door, I swung the bedroom door open just as my mother was about to knock. She stared at me with wide, surprised eyes.

"Yes?" I breathed, feeling a very unusual, slightly too-happy, smile entertaining my lips. She stayed silent for a moment longer, taking in my dishevelled look before pulling her hand back and fixing a suspicious stare on me.

"What were you doing? Do you have a girl in there?" She questioned, trying to peek over the top of my head with a disapproving curl to her lips. I swallowed, fighting back the attack of panic.

"No!" I blurted out too fast, in answer. I cleared my throat and started again. "No, I don't. Sorry, I was just...doing some exercises with Lee. Oh, Lee's here, by the way." I realised I was speaking too fast, trying to breathe and calm myself down.

"What is he doing here this late at night? Jake, what've I told you about having friends over on week nights?" Her eyebrows curved down and she placed an irritated hand on her hip. I desperately fought not to roll my eyes, thankfully coming out victorious.

"Problems at home and stuff. He's staying here for a couple of days until things settle down, if that's okay?" I placed my best pleading and sympathetic expression on my features. Her's softened in return and she sent me a gentle smile.

"Alright then, as long you behave together then that's fine." She turned to leave, and I was about to shut the door again before she swiftly turned back and said, "Don't leave the door unlocked and the alarms off again, Jake. Especially when you're upstairs. Your fathers not very pleased about that, so stay away from him tonight unless you want a lecture." With that, she sauntered off and I finally closed my door and collapsed on my bed with a huff of relief.

"Is it safe to come out yet?" I heard Lee whisper, looking towards him to find him peeking around the bathroom door. I nodded and he stepped out, his joggers securely fixed on his legs, but apparently he didn't care much for his shirt as that was nowhere in sight. "Bloody hell, bit uptight tonight isn't she?" He acknowledged, collapsing beside me. I didn't say anything in return, paranoid that she was listening in somewhere.

Instead I replied with, "That was close," in a small voice that sounded more as a realisation. "I don't know what they'd do if they found out, Lee. Probably kick me out onto the street and cut me off from my allowance."

"I don't think they'd do that," he attempted to reassure me, but his voice didn't sound very convincing. "At least your 'rents are still together." He added as an after thought. "'Least your dad isn't cheating on her with some whore from the office. Or maybe he is, guess you'll never know." I turned to look at him with an evident look of shock.

"Thank you, Felix, that's a comforting thought." He turned his head and gave me a sad smile, mouthing the words I'm sorry before sliding his fingers into my hair and leaning forward, just far enough to press his lips against mine in a gentle kiss.

Chapter 8

I have to say I wouldn't have thought it, but getting up and ready for school with Lee was a very awkward situation. When he started to strip off his clothes to hit the shower, I turned around and gasped like I hadn't seen his jewels before, blurted, "What the fuck dude?", and then face-palmed after realising why my reaction was so ridiculous. Of course the whole time this was going on, there was a massive smirk slapped on Lee's face.

He walked up to me in all his glory, tilted my head back by my hair and whispered over my lips, "You're acting like you haven't seen my dick before," then he released me, winked and disappeared into the en-suite. Leaving me tingling with arousal and a blush creeping onto my cheeks. Sighing, I finished drying my hair with a towel and tossed it into the corner of my room, by my door. This was going to take some getting used to.

I heard the water from the shower start to run and decided I didn't want to stick around for Lee to make more fun of me, whilst the only thing covering him and his wet body was a white towel. Oh God, way too tempting. I almost dived through the en-suite door and into the shower with him. But instead, I took the less sexier route of down the stairs and into the kitchen where I found my father reading the morning newspaper. As always.

"Son," my father greeted in his usual gruff tone, his eyes not straying from the words in his hands. Mandy was dancing about, placing a plate full of English breakfast in front of his poise form. "Thank you, Amanda." He muttered, folding his newspaper in half and placing it beside him. I perched on one of the other kitchen stools, a seat away from my father's position.

Mandy bustled her way over to me with a large grin, "Good morning mister Aston, what would you like for breakfast?" She winked as if to say, or have you already had it? I cringed and rolled my eyes. She seemed to understand our silent conversation, letting escape a slight chuckle. It annoys me when she calls me by my last name, but my mother doesn't approve of a maid addressing her employees on a personal level. However, she always does it when my parents aren't around.

"Is there some inside joke I'm not familiar with?" My father's voice pitched in, his tone surprisingly light, an unusual smile on his lips. Me and Mandy both shook our heads silently.

"I'll just have toast and butter today, thanks Mandy." She nodded and got straight on with it. My father's full attention then got turned on me, and I shifted in my seat awkwardly. "Something wrong, dad?" I avoided eye contact, chewing on the inside of my cheek.

He shook his head as if he was stuck in slow motion. "There's just something a little...different about you today." I swallowed nervously, my eyes now trained on the counter that I was tapping my fingers on in an off-beat rhythm.

"Really? I don't feel different." I lied. I felt entirely different. I didn't even feel like the same person anymore. Mandy placed the plate of toast in front of me, I nodded in thank and concentrated on eating it as slowly as possible so I constantly had a mouthful of food, and you're not supposed to talk with your mouth full, I thought.

Thankfully, he just made a hmm noise and turned back to his breakfast. For the duration of finishing my toast, all that was heard was the shuffling of Mandy and the clinking of knives and forks. I stood up to leave, grabbing an apple from the fruit bowl on my way out, and jogged my way back upstairs. I figured it was better looking at Lee naked, than staying in an awkward silence with my father.

To my disappointment, Lee was fully dressed spare for his top which he was just pulling over his head. His hair was left ruffled after he tugged his head through the shirts hole, letting the rest of the grey material slide down his torso without him even touching it.

He smiled at me before running his hands through his hair, straightening it out. He always left his hair natural, unstyled. He never needed to do anything with it, cause it looked good just how it was. I don't know how he deals with that fringe though, constantly swooping into his eyes all the time.

"You alright?" He asked me, which shook me out of my thoughts.

"What? Oh yeah, yeah I'm fine." Quickly tossing Lee the apple, I swiftly moved over to my mirror, instantly pulling a slanted face at the sight of my hair - which was sticking up in every which direction. Grabbing the tub of gel, I styled it how I normally do; girls love the fluffy, spikey hair look. Reasonably satisfied with the outcome, I perched on the edge of my bed where Lee was laying. "You?" I asked softly.

"Huh?" He jerked his face towards me with furrowed brows, taking a bite out of his apple with a crunch.

"Are you alright?"

"Oh, yeah am fine. You could make me better though," he chuckled, a smirk forming on his amused face. I rolled my eyes, making to get up but was stopped by a pressure on my wrist. Lee pulled me down until I was laying on my side, where we sorta swapped positions - as now, Lee was looming over me, climbing onto my body. He paused, reaching over to the bedside drawers and placed his apple gently on the surface, before settling back into place.

"Lee, we have school in half an hour," I protested, pressing my palms against his chest, but he didn't listen. He leaned down, kissing along my jawline softly. "Felix, seriously man, my parents are here. What if they-"

"They won't," he pinned my wrists by each side of my head, leaning in on my face so close my eyes couldn't focus on his properly. He brushed his bottom lip against my top, flicking his tongue out before fully taking my lips in his. I let out a slight whimper in surprise, but kissed him back nonetheless, letting my eyelids fall shut. The pressure of his fingers on my wrists grew tighter, pushing them harder into the mattress, allowing deeper access into my mouth.

"Lee, stop," I muffled, trying to turn my head to the side. Eventually, he released my wrists and sat back with a pout.

"Jake, come on, live a little." The corner of his lips twitched up into a smile that was just so damn sexy. I glanced towards the clock on the small table by my bed, and shook my head.

"We can't, I bet the driver's here already." I tapped him on the thigh in an indication to get up, which he obeyed with a loud, heavy sigh of disappointment. "Come on, grab your shit," I picked up my school bag from the floor at the bottom of my bed and heaved it over one shoulder, seeing Lee doing the same I headed on towards the door. He followed with heavy footsteps, trying to silently remind me that he wasn't impressed.

He continued the heavy footsteps until we reached the bottom of the stairs, where we were greeted with my father who, the lucky bastard, doesn't have to go into work until ten this morning.

"Hello Felix, it's been a while since I've seen you around here." He smiled in that unusual way again, like he was floating on cloud nine or something. I don't know, my parents have always been overly-weird.

"Mr. Aston," Lee greeted politely. "Yeah, home life's been a little crazy, but I've been told it's okay for me to stay around here for a while?"

"Absolutely!" My father's words practically sprung from his mouth. My eyes shot wide open and I just stared at him with complete bewilderment. "Anyway, your ride to school is waiting outside for you, so I suggest you head on out," we gave him a quick nod and I dragged Lee outside the front doors and into my chauffeur's sleek, black car like it was a life saving decision. After that, I took a moment to just breathe.

"Your dad seemed like he was on fuckin' happy pills. What the hell was up with his eyes, could they get any wider?" Lee laughed, and I had to let a small chuckle out too. But I was slightly worried after hearing the word pills. The rest of the car journey was spent mostly in silence, I was too preoccupied with keeping the past away from the front of my mind to really focus on starting up a conversation. Lee didn't seem to care, he was texting away on his phone anyway.

When the car finally pulled up outside the school gates, I slowly slid out the door in realisation that me and Lee would have to try and act normal again today. I rolled my eyes and lolled my head forward, watching my feet as they walked around the back of the car to join Lee on the sidewalk. I kept my head down until we were past the school entrance and into the halls that lead to our lockers. Lee branched off from my direction to go ditch his stuff in his own locker, whilst I continued ahead to mine.

Unlocking it, with only slight irritation after forgetting the code three times, I threw all the books I didn't need until after lunch inside, slammed the damn door shut and almost forgot about Lee completely as I walked straight on past him.

"Jake, hang on," he called, placing a hand on my shoulder in a way of slowing himself down after running towards me. His touch lingered a little too long, before sliding down the length of my arm and gently running over my hand. I chose not to bring it up, thinking that maybe he's always done that and maybe I've just never noticed it until now.

"Oh yeah, sorry. Was in a completely different place," I mumbled, still not really listening to anything he said. But I did hear him laugh and mutter something about me always zoning out a lot, after that I wasn't paying much attention.

We reached the sixth form room a couple minutes later, greeted in the usual fashion. I fixed a grin on my lips and kept my tone happy and light, hoping that was how I normally acted before all this shit happened between me and Felix. I saw Owen standing on his own by the window, sneakily puffing a cigarette. He was always pushing his luck inside the school building with shit like that. Gotta' love him for it though.

Walking over to him and silently leaning against the wall by his side, he turned his head to greet me with a nod whilst taking a drag of his cig. After sending a cloud of smoke out the window, he turned back to me and said, "Hey Jake, how're ye doin'?"

"I'm alright mate. You keep smokin' them things and you're not going to be too well in a couple of years though," I tell him this everyday, but it just goes in one ear and out the other.

"Aye," he chuckles, taking another inhale and pointing his hand over towards the other side of the room, where a bunch of girls were conversing. "Hey, ye see tha' lass o'er there, yeah? Her name's Tami. Ye see 'er, yeah?" I spotted a brunette girl standing just out of the circle, a few girls speaking to her but she didn't seem overly popular. I didn't recognize her face a bit, though.

"What about her?" I asked, intrigued.

"She just started t'day an I think am in-fuckin'-love wi' 'er, Jake," he chuckled again, but I could see a slight hint of a blush sneaking into his cheeks. I smacked him on the arm with the back of my hand.

"Fucking yeah right, Owen. More like you just want to get in her pants." I scoffed, rolling my eyes. "You can't be serious. You're in bed with girl one night, and the next with another. I'd fuckin' bet you couldn't keep faithful for one hour," I raised my eyebrows at him in humour, but he just laughed and agreed.

" 'Spose you're right. But I did 'ear a rumour goin' around tha' Bonnie Tyler was inta ye," he slipped me a wink, smirking. I bit my lip in thought, wanting to know exactly how much she was into me.

Chapter 9

English class was always a bore. I already knew my alphabet, so what was the use of it? The teacher was droning on at the front of the class about some poet - come on, a poet? We need to learn about some guy who has a knack for rhyming a bunch a words, or teaching a moral in the most head achingly-complicated way possible. That's fucked up. And boring.

So as a result of that, I never listened. Instead, I allowed my eyes to wander aimlessly around the cosey little classroom that held about twenty students in. Occasionally, my gaze would fall onto a few girls, one that was seemingly a regular was Bonnie Tyler. But I don't blame myself, she's a damn good sight.

Ever since year seven, Bonnie has always been the centre of attention - next to Kimberly Towson. But then again, they're the best of friends - so it seems only fitting, right? Though they couldn't look more different. Where Kimberly has golden blonde hair, to match her more-than-sweet personality; Bonnie has chocolate brown which goes with her dark, angry but strong personality. They're practically the complete opposite.

Thing about Bonnie is, she's so bad tempered that the slightest thing you do wrong, she'll kick off. But there's always been something about her that I liked - I don't know if it's just the fact that she could kick my arse, verbally and physically if I'm honest, that makes me attracted to her so much. I shrugged the thought away as I felt my phone vibrate in my pocket.

Making sure to look at it discretely, I read the text message from Felix: I heard the East building's toilets are always empty this end of the day;)

I stared at the screen for what seemed like half an hour before shaking my head and realising what he meant, replying with: Really, Felix? And you say I'm the slut.

I looked up from where I was sitting, finding Lee - who was sat three seats across from me - grinning like an idiot. I rolled my eyes in his direction and he turned his attention back to his phone.

But Jake, I can't stop thinking about your cock. An instant rush of arousal swept through my entire body as I read the last word, but I maintained my cool.

Before I could send a reply, the school bell was already ringing and the teacher dismissed us without hesitation. I quickly grabbed my books and shoved my pen in my mouth, heading for the door. I thought I'd escaped Felix but when my pen was snatched from between my teeth, I turned my head to find Lee smirking at me whilst waving my pen in between his thumb and forefinger.

"Can I have my pen back?" I said, dodging the rushing bodies that were heading in the opposite direction to me. I could see Lee concentrating on keeping up and not getting lost in the sea of people, from the corner of my eye. When we were finally outside and walking down to our next class, our pace slowed and he was back by my side in no time.

"How much does this pen mean to you?" His voice was teasing and sheepish. I rolled my eyes at him again.

"It's a thirty pence biro, Lee, I'm not gonna dive in front of a lorry for it." He chuckled before shoving his hand against my shoulder, forcing me against a wall. I was taken by surprise and quite thankful there was a building there to stop me from tumbling to the ground. "What now?" I sighed exasperatedly, looking about the area we were standing in. People were walking past us without even noticing we were there.

When I refocused back on Lee, my pen was resting against his bottom lip, pulling it down slightly. Tugging the corner of his lips up was a smirk, before half my pen disappeared into his mouth as his lips pursed around it. One of my brows raised on their own accord at the sight, and I fought to gain control of my eyes to stop them from staring.

He started sliding the pen in and out of his mouth slowly, that smirk still only just there. I swallowed and begged my eyes to pull my gaze away, but apparently they were enjoying the show a little too much. His shoulders shook with laughter as he pulled the biro from his mouth for the final time, his hand dropping down to my waist where he slipped the pen safely into my jean pocket.

"We should, uh, we should get to class." I muttered, shoving past him and fast-walking the rest of the way to Science.

I managed to keep away from Lee for the rest of the morning, but he caught up with me eventually by dinner time. So I decided to just stick around Chase, since Lee isn't stupid enough to do anything in front of him.

I felt a tap on my arm, finding Felix nodding in turn of asking if we can talk. I sighed, but obliged since I've been avoiding him all day. We walked over, away from the group of friends I was hovering by - not really listening to the conversation just using them as a shield from Lee's teasing - towards an empty part of the field where we stood awkwardly.

"How come you're dodging me?" I furrowed my brows as soon as I recognised the odd tone to his voice, realising that he was slightly hurt. I turned to face him fully.

"Look, Lee, you can't do that in school. I really don't need people finding out about this shit." He folded his arms across his chest and stared at me indignantly. "Stop looking at me like that," I said absently before intending to carry on about being discrete, but Lee interjected.

"Like what?" His tone was snarky, his brows set in a fine, pissed off line.

"Like that!" I gestured my hand towards his face. He shrugged in return. "Oh my God, you're like a child!" I blurted, throwing my hands up in exasperation.

"Yeah? Well you're a prick." He was just being petty now, and I wasn't about to start an insult war with him. And not because of the fact that he always wins, just because I'm really not in the mood. "You're so serious about everything. Why can't you just chill out?" I glared at him angrily.

"What the fuck? Just because I don't want people walking around the damn school thinking I'm," I paused, looking around for wandering eyes, moving closer and lowering my voice. "Thinking I'm gay." I finished in a mere whisper. Lee threw his head back in an arrogant laugh.

"Oh my God, you make me so God damn frustrated!" He balled his fists up at his side. "Dude, not that I'm trying to push this onto you or anything, but you can't fuck a guy - enjoy it - and then turn around and say you're not gay." His eyes softened and his features expressed humour. I didn't care, the only thing I was happy about was the fact that he didn't shout it for the whole school to hear.

"I like how you tell me this afterwards," I muttered unintelligently, more sarcastic than anything. "Just, lay off it when we're at school, yeah?" He huffed but nodded, a frown curling his lips. I gave him one last look before turning to leave, but Lee stopped me with a call of my name. I turned my head back in question.

"We need to talk about this tonight." I felt my brows knit together, but I agreed all the same. I made my way back over to the rest of the lads, leaving Felix standing on his own looking as if he was deep in thought. I don't know what there was to talk about, but I guess I'll soon be finding out.

"Hey," I heard Chase's voice by ear as he nudged me with his shoulder to gain my attention. I acknowledged him, directing my gaze away from Lee and onto his concerned face. "Something goin' on with you two?" He questioned, his brows furrowed.

"What, me and Lee?" He nodded. "Nah mate, he's just being immature." Chase made an 'O' shape with his mouth before we both walked over to join Owen, Tyler, Kev and Harry who were stood with a group of girls. One of those being Bonnie Tyler.

As we approached, I was able to hear the conversation they were all having. Tyler was the one speaking at the moment. "And so that's why girl-girl action is hot." I widened my eyes as I listened, wondering how in the hell they got onto that subject. Paranoia itched at the back of my head as I wondered if they knew...nah, I'm just being stupid. They're guys, it's what they talk about. It's what I talk about - cause I'm a guy, and I'm still into girls...so I must still be straight, right?

"What do you think, Jake?" I heard a familiar voice pull me out of my thoughts. When I looked up I found everyone's eyes aimed at me. I fidgeted underneath their stare and ran the question back through my mind. "About girl on girl action?" They all nodded and I cleared my throat. "Uh, yeah it's cool." I inwardly winced.

'It's cool' Jake, really? I thought whilst cringing. I tried to dive in and save myself. "I mean, you know, it's a bit awkward when you're asked by a girl, haha. But it's hot." I shrugged nonchalantly, but inside I was practically dying from embarrassment.

"I think it's pretty fucking sexy," Felix's voice bellowed from behind me. I strained my neck to look over my shoulder, seeing him approaching us and stopping in between me and Chase, directly in front of Bonnie. "So, if girl-girl action's hot for us guys, is it the same for you girls? You know...with boys." He quirked an eyebrow in Bonnie's direction.

She seemed to blush a dark shade of pink before biting her bottom lip and turning to look back at her friends, who were glancing to and from each other. They were all smiling, except for Kimberly who was looking at her younger brother in disbelief. I, on the other hand, wished I could just disappear, right now. I don't know what he's playing at, but he's so gonna pay for it later.

Chapter 10

I shoved Lee roughly through the door of my bedroom, slamming it shut behind me. Thankfully, I didn't have to worry about my parents over-hearing me, as they didn't get back from work for another couple of hours. So I let loose, with the question Lee had asked the girls back at school, still fresh in my mind.

"What the fuck was that, Felix?" I shouted, frustration securely evident in my tone. But Lee just raised his shoulders to shrug in innocence.

"What was what?"

"You damn well know what. What are you trying to do? Cause if you're just trying to piss me off, then you're doing a great fucking job of it!" My fist was itching to connect with his jaw, and my body begged for the release it would bring for the anger building up inside me. But for some stupid ass reason, I couldn't bring myself to hit him like I usually would have.

"I was just having a conversation, Jake," I could tell he was having a mental war trying to keep his lips from curving up into a playful smile.

"I'm glad you find it funny, Lee. Really, I am."

"Oh, chill out!" He huffed, striding towards me with a slightly amused expression. I stood my ground as he stopped barely an inch away from me, a smirk planted on his lips after he flicked his tongue out to wet them.

"You ever heard of personal space, Lee?"

"Shut up, you love it." His smirk transformed into a grin as his hands found my hips and he started gently pushing me backwards, steering me towards the wall by my door. But I wasn't done being angry with him, although I was finding it a little difficult to remember exactly why I was angry with him. It's like every time his eyes dragged themselves up and down my body, my brain was wiped clean of all coherent thoughts.

He began kissing along my neck as my head lolled back against the wall. "Besides," he whispered across my skin. "Guy on guy action is hot." I heard him chuckle quietly. I kicked my brain into gear and pushed him away from me, where he stumbled back with surprise.

"It's not a joke, Felix. If they find out that we're..."

"What? A little more than just friends?" He chuckled, an eyebrow raised in humour. I gave him a deadpan look, silently begging him to start being serious. After all, he was the one that said we needed to talk about this. And there I was, talking. Yet there he was, making a joke of it all.

After a fairly long staring contest, Lee eventually caved and thankfully, this time, he was more serious. "Okay, okay, fine." He held his hands up briefly. "So, maybe I got a little jealous." His shoulders shrugged once again.

"Jealous?" I asked him, confused.

"Don't even act like you weren't checking Bonnie Tyler out all day, today." Well, I got what I asked for. Serious Felix Towson. I kinda hoped he'd go back to joking around, cause the glare he was shooting my way, well, if looks could kill...

"I wasn't checking her out, Lee! Can a guy not appreciate-"

"Fuck off, appreciating is just the less common way of saying you were checking someone out! Don't bullshit me Jake, I know you. And I definitely know when you're eye-fucking someone."

"Oh yeah? And how would you know that?"

"Cause you've done it to me enough times for me to recognise it."

"What the- no I have not! Are you fucking kidding me?" I noticed my throat started getting dry and my cheeks started heating up. I was sure if I looked in a mirror, there would be an uncanny resemblance to Pikachu - minus the yellow skin. But you know what? It was completely unrelated to the conversation I was having right now. Completely unrelated.

"Look, whatever, forget it. I just wanna know if you take this thing between us seriously or not?" I squirmed underneath his stare.

"Well that's just it, Lee, a thing. That's all this is between us." I gestured between the two of us as I spoke. Felix took a step back, almost as if in surprise at hearing what I'd said.

"Just a thing. Right, fine, I get it." He muttered, almost inaudibly, but I managed to catch the words. Just.

"Come on Lee, you know I didn't mean it like that. But we're not exactly in a relationship either," I took a step forward, but barely noticing. "Guys can't really...be in a relationship. It's not right. I just- I gotta figure all this out in my head, Lee, I'm so fucking confused right now." I felt as if my sentences were jumbled up and what I'd said was just a bunch of nonsense, but I couldn't give two shits.

"So...what, then, Jake? I'm just here to give you a good time, is that it?" Hurt was evident, in the break of his voice and the moisture in his eyes. He wasn't crying, but he looked like he was on his way there.

"You're twisting my words now," I attempted in a calm tone, taking another step forward so we were only a few inches apart now.

"No I'm not, that's what you said. You said guys can't be in a relationship. We're not in a relationship so-"

"I never said I'm just using you for sex though did I-"

"Just? So what else are you using me for, Jake? Please do tell."

"Now you're just being stupid. You're twisting my words because you're upset-"

"Upset? Who said I was upset? You know what, just forget it Jake, I'm outta here." Before I could get anymore words out, Lee was slamming the door behind him. The thought of chasing after him reverberated inside my head for a while, but I fought against the urge and just collapsed down onto my mattress with a heavy sigh.

"That guy is gonna be the death of me," I murmured to myself with a groan.

After a couple of hours, Lee came back with one of those looks. You know, the guilty look, where they know they've stepped out of line and, maybe, been a little over sensitive. The look that clearly says: I know, I was a dick, and this is awkward for me but, forgive me? Without anyone even having to say a thing.

So with a nod of the head from me in answer, Lee breathed a sigh of relief and headed straight for the shower. By the time he was out, I was already dressed in my pajamas waiting to brush my teeth. Lee was merely dressed in a pair of briefs, but, thank God, they weren't the tight ones. You know, the ones that leave little or nothing to imagination. Cause fuck, my parents were only down the hall and with the sounds I made last time, they'd have no problem hearing us.

I spat the toothpaste into the sink and swilled my mouth out before heading to bed, flicking off the lights. Lee had already tucked himself in on his side of the bed, but he had a very disarming grin fitted onto his lips. As I slid under the sheets, I felt our bare arms brush against each other momentarily, but I decided against announcing the fact that tingles skittered through my body from the touch.

We laid there in the silence, darkness surrounding us both. But I could see Lee's face from the beam of yellow seeping through my curtains, from the outside lights. The grin was no longer there, and his eyes were focused on the ceiling. I watched the covers that were thrown over his chest, rise and fall in time with his breathing.

"Jake," his whisper sounded like a shout in the midst of the deafening silence, and his sudden voice made my whole body jolt in surprise.

"Yeah?" I whispered back. I listened to the sound his head made as it moved against the pillow when he turned to face me. Our eyes met and it felt like the whole world froze for a single second as we gazed at each other. But that's stupid, and something a pansy teenage girl would say, so I brushed the thought aside and made a deal never to ever think that again.

"I'm sorry." He said, simply, before I felt his fingers run over my stomach and up to curve around the back of my head as he slid closer, rolling fully onto his side now.

"For what?" I could feel the pads of his fingers drawing circles and toying with the hair at the base of my neck. My eyes slid shut from the sensation, and I felt my whole body relax into his touch.

"You know," I'm sure I heard the sound of him licking his lips as he moved even closer, and I'm sure I felt the brush of his nose against mine. But I didn't want to open my eyes, I couldn't. "For throwing a bitch fit. I mean, it's not like one day you're gonna wake up and never look at another girl again." He chuckled lightly, but managed to keep it low. Which somehow, made my breathing speed up. I don't know, that chuckle was somehow incredibly sexy.

"It's okay, Lee." I heard the sound of the duvet as he moved underneath it, and felt his body press up against mine. Chest to chest, with out foreheads resting against each other. "I shouldn't have said some of the things I did." I opened my eyes then, or it was more like they threw themselves open, wanting to watch his expression as I said my next words.

Licking my lips, I took a deep breath and said, "It's not just a thing to me, Lee. But you know I'm not good with my feelings and...I don't like, you know, being open. It's hard for me to admit, but I- I don't know. I guess, what I'm trying to say is, I'm willing to..." I could feel the embarrassment building up from the tips of my toes to the hairs on my head.

My cheeks grew hot and I twiddled my thumbs between our bodies, the backs of my fingers pressed up against Lee's stomach, so he felt every single movement they made. "Fucks sake," I said under my breath. But I caught the sight of Lee smirking, which meant he'd obviously heard it. "Okay, can I ask you a question?" I decided to do this a different way, as discussing the way I felt was clearly too difficult for my lips to even remotely say the words.

"Yeah, what is it?" I took a deep breath, mentally preparing myself for what I was about to ask. I couldn't believe I was going to do this. I couldn't believe what I was about to ask my best friend. I mean, it shouldn't have been that much of a shock to me but, I'd never done this before. It was really fucking nerve wracking.

"Lee," deep breath. "Will you be my boyfriend?" I hadn't realised my eyelids had closed once again, until I felt Felix's lips press against mine in a gentle kiss. They opened just as Lee was pulling back, to find him smiling. I waited for him to say something, but he just bit his bottom lip.

It was then that I knew the kiss was his way of saying yes, and I couldn't stop the grin that broke out onto my lips as I rolled over onto my other side. And I swear, even when I fell asleep, the smile stayed there for the entire night.

Chapter 11

"You two are unusually chirpy this morning," I heard Chase's voice rumble through my ears. I was currently in the middle of laughing my ass of at...well, I really don't remember what made me laugh. The important thing is, I was in a very good mood today. I spun on my heels and threw an arm around Chase's shoulders, pulling him in for a quick hug.

I sighed before saying, "I'm just having a really good day today," I took note of the slight dreaminess of my voice, and usually I would have been very embarrassed, but I couldn't really care.

"Yeah-huh. More like you got lucky last night." Chase scoffed, pulling away from me to eye me with suspicion. "So tell me, Jake, who was it?" His brows wiggled in encouragement, but I just chuckled and walked away. Then I heard, "Holy shit, you did get lucky last night!" And Chase was right by my side once more.

I gave him a sideways glance, rolling my eyes. "Can a guy not be happy, just because he's in a good mood?"

"Yeah, a guy can. But Jake Aston can't. At least, not as happy as this." He eyed me again, only this time the suspicion was replaced with concern. "Are you feeling all right? Need to go see the school nurse? Have a lie down? A drink of water?"

"I'm fine, Chase." I tried to force boredom into my tone, but it just came out as light and carefree as ever. When we stopped walking, I found that we were now surrounded by a large group of our friends. Owen and Felix were standing next to each other, smirking and grinning after a few things they'd said.

Just as I was about to look away, Lee's gaze flitted up to meet mine and he gave me a small smile. I swear it was like he had a radar that went off inside his head every time I looked at him. As if my feet had a mind of their own, they walked over to Lee's side and my shoulder seemed to nudge him playfully.

Okay, now I know what Chase means. I'm not myself today. What the fuck is going on? I just nudged Felix with a look plastered on my face that, probably, resembled a loved-up teenage girl staring at a Robert Pattinson poster. I shivered at the thought. I needed to get a hold of myself before someone starts suspecting something. Though I think Chase was already onto me.

"Do you know, I don't think you've stopped smiling since you arrived, Jay." A voice pitched in from the crowd of people, which me and Lee apparently stood in the centre of. I couldn't pick out exactly who'd said it, I didn't even recognise the voice. So I just laughed it off, and tried to tone my happiness down. Jeez, if I got any happier I was gonna be walking around with a hard-on all day.

"He got lucky last night!" Chase shouted out to the crowd of guys, a large grin imprinted on his face. The crowd cheered in return, like it was some sort of accomplishment. I wanted to say I didn't, but hey, if they wanna think I did then it's doing no harm to my reputation.

The school bell rang out, filling our ears with the most excruciatingly painful sound you'd ever heard, and with a groan we all started to make our way towards our third period lessons. Me and Lee walked towards Maths together, since our rooms were up the same staircase.

He leaned into my ear and said, "You're grinning like the Cheshire Cat," I didn't need to look at his face to know he was smirking, smugly. I jabbed my elbow into his side and he let out a girlish giggle before locking an arm around my neck and pulling my head down. He was practically dragging me to class by my neck, which caused me to stumble over my feet over a dozen times, while I was making weird noises of disapproval and snide remarks.

When he finally released me, I smacked him round the back of the head playfully, and he returned the favour. "You're such a dick, Lee." I stated, still smiling.

"Yup, a dick you like to suck. Ohhh!" He put his hands around his mouth and cheered himself on for his comeback. I couldn't help the chuckle, and I couldn't exactly deny what he'd said either. I opted to keep quiet and just smile it off, much like I'd been doing with everything that day.

When it was time to go into class, we went in our opposite directions with a quick, "See you after Maths." And a wink on Lee's behalf.

It was dinner after Maths, which me and Lee decided to spend on our own. We walked the short distance into town at a leisurely pace. Barely anyone could be arsed to go into town after two years of being allowed to. The newness wore off and now everyone stayed on site for lunch, so the walk there was quiet with barely anyone around, which gave me and Lee a bit of time to talk without the fear of being overheard.

"So, what's got you so happy?" Felix finally asked after a long moment of silence. It wasn't an awkward silence though, in fact, I felt at ease. I closed my eyes against the sun that was burning down on my skin, heating my body up. Thankfully, I'd left my jacket and bags in school so I wasn't sweltering from the warmth.

"Dunno really," I answered simply, my voice soft and calm.

"You're not on shrooms are you?" I slid my eyelids open slowly, rolling my head to the right to point a humoured gaze in his direction. I knew what he meant. I was tilting my head towards the sky with my eyes closed, and the cause of that was not walking in a straight line. So yeah, I probably looked like I was drunk or, in Lee's opinion, stoned.

He nudged me, and even though it was gentle, it sent me stumbling over my feet sideways. I decided I'd keep my eyes open from then on. "What are you thinking about?" His tone sounded thoughtful itself, and I shrugged even though I was going to answer him.

"I'm thinking about..." I was going to say something completely different to what I said next, and I won't even admit to myself that I even contemplated telling him. "Chips."

"Chips?"

"Yeah, chips. With chip spice and salt...but no vinegar. I hate vinegar."

"But I love vinegar," I shot him a glare.

"If we're sharing, there will be no vinegar. I'm the man in this relationship, so everything goes my way." I joked as I always did, but then realised the half-truth of what I'd just said. I asked him to be my boyfriend last night, and completely forgot about it until now.

"I thought it was the woman that always got what she wanted?" He winked sheepishly with a grin tugging at the corners of his lips.

"Nah, that's overrated." I replied, waving him off lazily. He laughed lightly for a moment before our conversation fell back into silence, but that was because we had now arrived at the town centre, which was always busy. We dodged the oncoming traffic of people, making our way to the best chip shop in town.

Stuart's Chip Shop, was what the big, green sign read. His chips were seriously like a taste of Heaven. They were just...amazing. It wasn't as busy as I thought it would have been, like it usually is, so we were in and out in a matter of minutes. Lee had given in after a quick squabble over the vinegar, and let me have my way.

"Where do you wanna sit?" He asked me as we lingered outside the chip shop's entrance.

"Park," I replied back over the chatter of nearby crowds. He nodded and started leading the way. We got there quite quick, to find that it was completely empty. The field was huge, with trees surrounding the outskirts. At the top, there was a children's playground, but we chose to sit at the bottom which was just a large area of empty field.

We chose a spot in the sun and laid down on our backs as we started digging into our chips. I pointed up towards the sky, at a certain cloud. "Looks like a Dinosaur," I said, tilting my face towards Felix to see if he'd seen it, grabbing another chip while I was at it.

"Oh yeah, a T-Rex innit?" I nodded in reply, tossing the chip in my mouth. Felix's eyes met in line with mine and they stayed there for a moment, just staring at me. Then in one sudden, energetic movement, Lee was straddling my waist.

"Woah, Lee, what are you doing? Someone might see!" I panicked, pushing at his chest, trying to get him off me.

"No they won't, chill out." He pushed me back down, his head hovering mere centimetres from mine with a chip sticking out from between his lips, now. I looked at it, feeling cross-eyed. His lips curved around it, into a smirk as he took in my confusion. He nodded his head at me in encouragement.

I sighed, quickly glancing around the area to see if anyone was there. Satisfied that the coast was clear, I leaned up. Just as I was about to close my mouth around it, Lee pulled away and sat back on his heels, spitting the chip out onto the ground with a laugh.

"Are you kidding me? You can't do that with a chip, that would be weird." I furrowed my brows at him.

"Well then why start doing it in the first place?"

"I just wanted to see if you would actually do it," he laughed again. I realised then, that I'd never make sense of Felix Towson. He leaned down and, without giving me time to stop him, kissed me. It was brief and soft, but still a kiss. In a public place. But honestly, I couldn't care less at that moment. I was still trying to work out exactly how his thought process worked.

"Well, we should head back to school." He said, clambering to his feet and picking up the near-empty chip box. I stood up and his hand instantly landed on my shoulder. I looked at it gingerly. "Thanks for the lovely date, Jake."

"Date?" I questioned him incredulously. He winked, smirked and then gave me his back as he walked away. Dick.

Chapter 12

"Come on," Lee pulled me by my jumper, leading me round to the back of West Building where it was basically deserted, and pushed me up against the wall. I gasped as my back hit the bricks. It's been a week since I asked him to be my boyfriend, and everyday for the past week Lee has managed to find at least one moment in the day to have a quick make out session. But today I sort of had this really bad feeling that I just couldn't shake.

"Lee, what're you doing?" I felt my bag's strap slide down my shoulder, and I struggled to pull it back up so it wouldn't fall. I could feel Lee's bumping against my thigh each time he moved.

"What? No one's around. And I've been dying to do this all day." He grinned against my mouth before his hands found my hips and pushed themselves underneath the waistband of my jeans. I tried to object but I was silenced by his lips on mine, and before I knew it I was lost in his kiss as my hands were lost in his hair. I felt his hands slide lower until he was cupping my ass and pulling me up against him.

His mouth trailed down my jawline and he licked his way up and down my neck before sucking on my earlobe eagerly. My head lolled back against the wall as my eyelids slid shut, granting Lee more access to my neck and he didn't hesitate in showing his thanks. I completely forgot about the world, nothing else existed outside of Lee's touch and I never wanted to return to reality.

But all good things must come to an end, I thought bitterly. Paranoia soon made itself known, with my eyes closed I couldn't see if anyone had wandered into the area and spotted us making out. I had this horrible feeling that we were being watched though, but I couldn't find the sense to check. My thoughts couldn't travel far from the fact that Lee was biting my neck - and no, not like a vampire, like a fucking sex God that knew exactly how to turn someone on.

Finally I forced my eyes to open, and they quickly scammed the area in front of me, luckily no one was there. But that was until I angled my head to the right. My heart jumped in my chest, did a few panicked twirls before sinking down into my stomach and making me feel sick. I stood there in shock, whilst Lee was continuing to grope me, obviously not having noticed we'd been caught.

I didn't know what else to do it was my instant reaction to pull away, but I couldn't because I was the one pushed up against the wall. So I pushed Lee away by the shoulders, and he stumbled back, almost ending up on his ass but he managed to balance himself out in time. I was panting heavily; a mix between being aroused and being on the verge of a panic attack.

There, standing at the corner of the building with his eyes wide to the point where it almost looked unnatural, was Chase. Fuck my shitty fucking life up the fucking arse, I shouted inside my head, only just holding myself back from screaming it out loud. This was a bad situation, this was a very bad situation. So what do I go and say?

"Hi Chase," oh, and I also waved. I waved. I just got caught making out with my best friend - who, by the way, has a dick - and I waved! Who the fuck does that? Facepalm. Chase didn't reply though, I don't even know what I expected him to say. But instead, he just sort of furrowed his brows before turning and leaving. He just left. Without a word.

"Holy shit, Lee!" I faced Felix with one helluva pissed off expression. I even think he stumbled back a little from the force of it. "Fuckin' careless! I told you not to do anything in school, why do you never listen to me?"

"Okay, firstly, don't act like you weren't enjoying it. Secondly, I love how this is automatically my fault. And thirdly, it's not even that much of a big deal!" He made large gestures with his hands to accompany his words.

"Not that much of a big deal? Lee, Chase just saw us make out! How is that not a big deal?" I screamed, and only afterwards realised I should probably keep my voice low in case someone walked by. Not that it would matter, the whole school probably knew by now. "He's gonna tell everybody. Fuck!"

"Come on, Jake, this is Chase we're talking about. He won't say a word. I'll talk to him later and sort things out." I rolled my eyes at him. How could he be so damn calm about this? I really didn't need the whole school finding out I've been having it off with my best friend. I don't know what was worse, the entire school knowing, or my parents. It's not like I could choose one over the other anyway.

"How're you going to do that? Did you see his face? He looked fuckin' disgusted."

"Actually, he just looked surprised. You're making this worse than it actually is." I was about to have another bitch fit at him but he held his hands up in turn of telling me to be shut up. "I said I'd sort it, Jake. So just fuckin' chill out, take a breath and go to class." I eyed him with frustration, but did as he told me anyway. I stormed off to my next lesson without a backward glance.

When I walked into the classroom, I suddenly felt self-conscious. No ones eyes instantly landed on me as I entered, thankfully, so I guess that was good news. But that still didn't ease my fear, and my fear was only encouraged as I saw Chase slip into the room and take his seat at the back of class. I focused my sight at the front board. The teacher hadn't arrived yet, so everyone was gathered in groups, lounging around on the desks and talking loudly.

Felix didn't have this class with me, which really sucked as I would've felt a lot better if he was here with me. I don't know why, but he suddenly seemed like he was my security blanket. I always found myself wanting to have him around, but when I think about it, it's always been like that. If ever I felt scared or something really bad happened, Lee would be the first person I'd go to. I wouldn't even have to think about it.

I didn't even notice that the chair beside me had become occupied, until I was nudged gently and a soft, "Hey Jake," was murmured by my ear. I almost jumped at the sound, I was so lost in thought. I turned my head just enough to see who was sitting next to me, and I was almost surprised I didn't tell by the voice.

"Hey Bonnie," I smiled with a playful wink. She brushed her fingers through her hair, ruffling her dark locks up a bit before sending a grin my way, that made her eyes sparkle with glee. "You okay?" I asked her, out of politeness.

"Yeah, bit tired. Can't wait for dinner, I hate mornings, always prefer the afternoon." She half-shrugged at the end of her sentence, then adding, "You?"

"Ah come on, you're sat next to me, this lesson can't be too bad," I winked again, cocking an eyebrow this time as well. "And yeah, I'm good. How can I not be?" I nodded towards her, biting my lip in a way which I hoped was subtle.

"Very true." Was all she said. Her glossy lips glimmering in the lighting as she pouted, looking as if she was chewing the inside of her cheek. She didn't half make it look sexy though. "We should hang out sometime, you know?" She said just as the teacher entered the room, with a clap of her hands to catch the students attention. Everyone instantly fell silent and quickly headed for their seats.

I leaned in towards her ear, feeling her hair brush gently against my cheek as I whispered, "We definitely should." My hand was beneath the table, tapping my mobile against her knee. She caught the hint and took it, deftly typing in her number before handing me my phone back. I could see her smiling from behind her hair that fell over her shoulders and shielded half her face from view, either side.

We sat in silence for the majority of the lesson, listening to Miss droning on at the front of the class as we took notes on what she was saying. Occasionally me and Bonnie would mutter something to each other, usually it involved mocking Miss O'Leary in some form or other. Even though I was enjoying myself, surprisingly Bonnie isn't actually boring company, I was grateful to hear the bell go for the end of lesson.

I gathered all my stuff and shoved it into my bag, throwing it over my shoulder and said a quick goodbye to Bonnie, who then joined her group of friends. It was just my luck that I'd pretty much literally bump into Chase as I tried to run for the entrance. I don't know why I was in a hurry, but I soon wished I'd have slowed down a little bit, so I didn't have to endure the awkwardness of a silent staring contest in the hall outside the classroom door.

Well, it wasn't completely silent as the banter of our classmates filled up the small space we stood in as they wandered past us without even glancing in our direction. It was as if we were invisible, but that's just how I liked to be in situations like this, so I had no complaints. Chase was just watching me though, I couldn't read his expression properly, but I could tell he was panicking a little. I don't blame him, what exactly do you say after discovering two of your best friends are gay?

"Look, Chase," I decided to be the first to initiate conversation. "I can explain everyth-" I cut myself off when Chase stumbled a few steps backwards, his eyes flitting to and from passerbyers. His head was shaking as he spun on his heels, turning to leave just as he had at the corner where he'd caught us. "Chase! Can we just talk?" I shouted after him, but he just kept on walking, not faltering for a second. I was beginning to dread school already.

Chapter 13

Chase avoided me for the rest of the day, he didn't return my calls or answer my texts. So in layman's terms, I was officially screwed. I told Lee this as we walked towards the car after school, I argued with him in muffled whispers in the back seat about it, and I even told him to go fuck a cow at some point. But he still insisted on thinking he could sort it out. You know what, I wish him luck. Chase didn't seem to be 'coming around' any time soon, that's for sure.

Yet I continued to whine and bitch and moan to him as I slammed my bedroom door shut and threw myself, face first, into my mattress. My words were muffled as I said, "My life sucks ass." I realised how ironic that sentence was after I'd heard Lee try to stifle a laugh. I turned to face him with my eyebrows low.

"Sucks ass..." he managed to churn out between the giggles.

"What? We're back in primary school now, are we?" I grabbed one of my pillows and launched it at him, he just stood there as it hit him in the face before succumbing to gravity and falling to the floor. His expression barely changed, except for becoming less amused and more playful. "Oh no, no. I know that look, and just no, Lee."

I held my index finger out towards him, fuck I don't know, maybe I expected myself to have magic freezing powers or something. Anything to keep him from doing what I knew he was going to do.

"Primary school, hey?" He cocked a golden eyebrow, taking agonizingly slow steps. I shuffled further up the bed, a feeble attempt to put some distance between us. Then, as sudden as the change in English weather, he pounced on the bed and pinned me down. He left no moment for me to breathe before he began the most cruel torture anyone could ever have to endure.

He started tickling me.

I giggled, high-pitched and girly - yep I went the whole nine yards of being a complete and utter chick when I was tickled. I tried to push his hands away from my sides, where his fingers were incessantly jabbing me in a way that made my body shiver. My stomach was beginning to hurt from all the laughing, but it wasn't a joyful laugh, it was a 'oh my fucking God, get the fuck off me before I kill you' laugh. See, back in primary, me and Lee used to have tickle wars. I don't know how it started, it was one of those things that just were.

"Okay, okay!" I breathed. "I give up, you win, or whatever. Just stop." I heard him laugh before collapsing down by my side and releasing a content sigh. The room settled into silence as I caught my breath.

"I always win." I turned my head to glare at him, but found myself just staring. Taking in the way his skin glowed in the yellow lighting of my room. The way when he closed his eyes, his eyelashes curved against his cheek. And, when they opened, how they just seemed to watch the view above him as if he weren't seeing a plain white ceiling; but as though he was looking out into the stars, into the universe. And I swear, if I watched closely, I could see the world glimmering inside his eyes.

Then he looked at me. And my breath caught in the back of my throat. I felt like I was watching us from above when my hand began to slide across the space between us, grabbing onto his shirt and pulling him towards me, holding on tightly. His forehead pressed against mine, our noses touching, our eyes staring. The only sound was of our breathing, mingling together between us each time we exhaled, in perfect sync. I briefly imagined the world spinning to a stop, everyone else freezing in time, leaving only us, only our moment still in motion. The thought sent a shiver down my spine.

"I know it hasn't been long since we started this, Jake." His voice sounded husky, a noticeable tremble as he spoke. "But I know when I'm sure about something." I stayed silent, waiting for him to make sense of what he was saying. I don't know if it was just me being stupid, but I wasn't quite catching on. "And I'm sure about this."

"What do you mean?" Our lips were so close, if I shuffled the slightest bit forward they'd be touching. Until this point, that was the only thing I could think about, but now I wanted to pull away. Put some distance between us. Because I couldn't believe what I was hearing. Most people would feel eager in anticipation for the next words, but me, no. I wasn't. Do I know why? I've said it before, and I'll say it again: I can't handle all this emotional shit. It's too overwhelming, too deep. But you know something that surprised me? I didn't run away.

I stayed long enough to hear, "I love you, Jake." Being whispered through his lips. I stayed long enough to watch as his eyes slid shut, expecting the worst reaction. Expecting me to shove him away and dive for the door. I know this, because I know Lee. I know that look on his face, where he presses his eyes closed so tightly in dread, where he wishes he could just sink away into the ground and never have to face reality. Where he wishes everything could just be a dream.

I stayed long enough to tilt his chin up, give him a cocky one-sided grin, and say, "Damn right you do." Before pulling our lips together and getting lost in the feeling of just having him close. The entire time, I noticed my grip on his shirt hadn't loosened one little bit. His palm rested against the back of my neck, slid down over my shoulder and stopped by my hip to pull me even closer, before returning to my neck and sliding into my hair. Just as I was about to roll him onto his back and crawl on top of him, I heard a knock on my door.

What surprised me again is, I didn't launch myself off the bed and over to the furthest wall, but instead, sat upright, rolled my eyes, sighed and then dragged myself over to see who had the nerve to interrupt us. Turns out, it was Mandy. I don't know who else I thought it would've been, my parents were both still at work. First thing I received from her was a huge grin as her eyes trailed from my face and over to the background, which by the little glint in her eyes was Felix laying on my bed with the covers all ruffled up and- Oh my God!

In an act of realisation mixed with complete shock and horror, I pushed Mandy backwards and slammed the door shut behind me, so it was only me and her stood out in the hall. She stared at me, her eyebrows raised so high on her forehead, it looked like she'd just had botox.

"It's not what you're thinking." I pointed at her, panic washing over my former relaxed state. "Wait- what're you thinking? Cause if you're not thinking what I think you're thinking, then you should keep thinking that." The words flew from my mouth so fast that I could barely understand what I'd said myself. Mandy just nodded along as if she knew what I'd said, but it was clear she didn't from the look on her face.

"I just wondered if you boys were hungry. I can make you sausage and mash?" She couldn't hold back a little snort at her pun. Honestly, it made me cringe with embarrassment.

"Look lady," I stood in her direct view, trying to make sure I had her full attention and she heard me clearly. I thought up some proper good words that would make her cower at the very sight of me...until her eyebrows dropped low and knitted together, so much so it looked like she'd miraculously formed a monobrow, and her lips curved down in disappointment. I immediately changed what I was going to say, cause I'm telling you now, this woman angry is like the terminator on steroids.

"I think sausage and mash sounds great!" I feigned excitement and gave her an innocent smile, it always used to win her over when I was a kid. By the looks of things, it still had the same effect, as her features softened and a smile sprung back onto her face.

"Excellent!" She gave me a cute shrug of the shoulders and turned to leave.

"Wait, Mandy," I took a few steps towards her as she twirled to face me. "Don't tell the 'rents, yeah?"

"Jake, honey, I still haven't told your parents about the time you spilt milk over their two thousand pound rug, when you were eleven."

"You know about that?" My voice dropped to a whisper, like I thought my parents would hear me from all the way in their offices if I spoke too loud. Mandy just smiled, nodding her head.

"Mandy sees all." She brought her index and middle finger up, pointing to her eyes before aiming them at mine, doing the 'I'm watching you' gesture. Well, that was one way to make me feel paranoid. "Relax Jake, your secret's safe with me. But I just want you to know that if you ever need to ta-"

"No!" I cut her off as soon as I caught on to what she was getting at. "Mandy, no...you're not giving me the birds and the bees talk. Please, not you." I pushed her by the shoulders, turning her around and directing her towards the stairs. "You go...do your shiz, me and Lee are just gonna chill out..." She peered over her shoulder at me, giving me that knowing and suggestive look. "I said chill out Mandy, not make out."

She held her hands up in surrender. "Okay then, you boys have fun." I could just imagine her winking as she sauntered on down the stairs. I slowly made my way back into my bedroom, finding Lee leaning against the wall right next to the door.

"Anybody ever tell you not to eavesdrop?" I muttered. He shrugged lazily with a smile.

"So, how bout we make out- I mean chill out, then." He winked playfully, taking my hand and pulling me over to the bed.

Chapter 14

"Gooood morning, sunshine!" My eyes fluttered open to the annoyingly cheery voice of Lee, only to feel surprise jolt through my body as I launched myself to the other side of the bed in an attempt to get away from his face, which was merely a centimetre from mine a minute ago.

"What- what the- what the hell, Felix?" He chuckled heartily before kneeling on the bed, at the area I was previously enjoying my sleep in.

"You know it's like almost twelve already, right?" My eyes shot towards the alarm clock on my bedside table, proving Lee's words true.

"Yeah, so? It's a Saturday. Saturday's always lazy day." He waved his slender index finger at me, patronisingly.

"Sunday is always lazy day; Saturday is fun day!" He grinned widely, sounding and looking like a five year old kid on Christmas morning. "Now come on, get up! We gots fun stuff to do." The grin never left his face. It was unnerving, really. But I obliged, dragging myself out of bed and into the bathroom to turn the shower on.

Just as I was about to pull my pants down, Lee waltzed straight in without any warning.

"Felix! What the hell, get out!" But he just leaned against the door frame, crossing one ankle over the other and smiled shamelessly.

"Come on, Jake, seriously?"

"Just because you've already seen this," I slid a hand down my stomach in mock tease. "Doesn't mean you get to see it all the time." Lee threw a pout my way, so I threw a towel his, which hit him straight in the face and he stumbled back a little from the force. He tossed it to the floor and pointed a scowl in my direction.

"I've done more than just see it," I heard him mutter under his breath. I chose to ignore the comment.

"Get out," I pointed to the doorway. He sighed dramatically, but obeyed nonetheless, slouching towards the door and shutting it behind him.

I showered pretty quick, finally got dressed and headed back into my room whilst towel-drying my hair. Lee wasn't anywhere to be found, so I figured he'd gone downstairs. Or he was hiding underneath my bed...I didn't bother to check.

After drying my hair and styling it, I threw a leather jacket over my shirt and jogged down the stairs to find Lee sitting on the sofa, chatting to my dad. I watched them with a look of bewilderment, eyeing my enthusiastic father and my cheerful best friend-slash-secret boyfriend with suspicion. Something was very wrong here. Why are they talking like they're best pals? In fact, why're they talking at all?

Ah shit, it's an omen. Was this the end of the world?

I walked slow, as if I was walking into a war zone and had to tread carefully, no misplaced footsteps or something might explode. My fathers eyes snapped to mine as soon as I took that first step closer, edging towards the kitchen where I was sure I'd find Mandy.

"Afternoon, Jake," he greeted with a wide, slightly fear-inducing, smirk on his lips. I lazily waved my hand in his direction as a return 'hello' and shuddered at the sight of Lee grinning at me. I briefly wondered if he was plotting something, like the scheming git he is.

"Felix, you uh, do you wanna...?" I nodded my head towards the kitchen's direction, indicating him to follow me in.

"Oh, yeah, sure," he nodded a goodbye to my father before joining me at my side as we walked towards the kitchen. "Your father's great," he beamed a smile my way. I eyed him a little cautiously, leaning away from him.

Mandy was dancing about the kitchen in her usual fashion. That was...until she saw me and Felix walk into the room. Her eyes turned mischievous and daring, a quirk to her lips that left me slightly unnerved. I made an immediate u-turn, yanking Lee around with me and headed for the games room, instead.

"What was that look for?" Lee chuckled, slinking into the sofa and instantly grabbing the xbox controller. I sat on the floor, next to Lee's feet.

"Everyone's acting really creepy today," I looked as far back as I could, the back of my head resting against the sofa, to see Lee's expression. He was fully focused on the screen in front of us. "You know, with the grinning and the eyebrows. I mean, you!" I exclaimed, pointing a finger at him. "You were talking to my father! Smiling at my father. You said he was great! It's a bad sign, surely."

"I think you're just being paranoid," he muttered, attacking the buttons on the controller angrily. "You were dreaming last night," he said, a smile curving one side of his lips.

"Really? That's amazing," Lee rolled his eyes at my sarcasm. I was a little annoyed that'd he'd changed the subject to that. We had a possible apocalypse on our hands, and he wanted to talk about me having a dream.

"You talked in your sleep. It was so cute that I was tempted to record it, but it was too cold to move outta the bed."

"I'd have killed you if you'd recorded it."

"Why?" He chuckled.

"Cause that's right fuckin' weird,"

He laughed a little louder. "Do you wanna know what you said?" His eyes momentarily found mine, fingers pausing on the controller. He had an element of glee snaking into his features.

"What?" I asked, admittedly a tad hesitant to find out by the way he was staring at me. He paused his game, sliding down from the sofa so he was kneeling beside me.

"Just that, erm," he leaned in towards my ear, dropping his voice to a deep murmur. "Just that you loved me." It took a moment for the last few words to register, before I was elbowing Lee in the side and watching him keel over himself on his back.

"Liar," I said, kicking him in the shin just for the fun of it. Lee was laughing, trying to say something between each chuckle. Once he'd sat back up, the evidence of his humour dissipated until it was only a small smile sitting on his lips.

"How do you know I'm lying? You weren't the one awake."

"Yeah, yeah," I waved him off, grabbing the discarded controller on top of the sofa. "Did I also mutter something about Tiffany boxes and rose petals?" I mocked.

"Yes, you did actually," he said, falling against my shoulder with the last remaining remnants of a laugh.

"Mhm, I'm sure," I grinned down at him, nudging him off me, but that only caused him to shift even closer. Eventually, he rested his head in my lap, laying on his back as I stared up at the screen. My hands were busy with the controller, playing the game almost like I was on autopilot, because my mind was otherwise focused on the gentle patterns Lee's finger was tracing against my chest.

"You remember just a few weeks back, when we used to just tease each other," his finger continued tracing a circle in the centre of my chest, over and over. "Did you ever used to think about me? You know, think about this. How we are now."

"Why're you asking?"

"Random question that popped into my mind." There was a short pause before he said, "I did...in case you were wondering." His hand stopped drawing circles and he crossed his arms across his chest. I'd completely forgotten about the game I was playing, fingers sitting idly on the buttons as I stared down at Lee in thought.

"What do you mean think about it?"

"You know, think about what it would be like to actually date. To...act all couple-y. Like you would with a chick or whatever." I placed the controller on the floor, leaving my arms by my sides.

"Not really. I never really thought about having a relationship with you."

"So all you thought about was the sex," he grinned, raising his brows. He didn't sound surprised at all. "I don't blame you, I'm a very sexy man." I smiled, inwardly agreeing with him. Lee's hand slid around the back of my neck, pulling himself up for a soft kiss.

When we parted, my eyes instantly found the open doorway, making sure no one had seen. Lee's eyes followed mine once I looked back, realisation setting in. "Sorry, forgot about your dad," he said, sitting up and leaning back against the sofa. "Pisses me off that we have to be careful, though."

"I know,"

"So why don't we just tell people?" There was a sudden burst of frustration in his tone. Like he was stuck inside a box and just wanted to break out, and I was the one stopping him from doing just that.

"Because, Felix, I can't. I don't think people would like it."

"Who gives a fuck about what people think!"

"I do."

"There's always going to be haters, Jake. Can't hide yourself forever. That's no way to live."

"Please don't turn into a bloody psychologist again, Lee. You've got that tone of voice and I really don't wanna sit and listen to it. Anyway, have you spoken to Chase yet?" I'd forgotten about Chase knowing, a little glad of the fact that Lee had reminded me.

"Nah, not yet. I'll see him on Monday."

"Man," I dropped my head into my hands. "He's one of my best friends. I really hope this hasn't fucked things up between us."

"He'll be fine, Jake," I wanted to believe that, but I couldn't. That was one of the main reasons why I didn't want people finding out about me and Lee. I didn't want everyone to start treating me differently. I just really hoped Chase hadn't told anyone.

"Yeah, let's hope." I mumbled, sighing. "I don't wanna talk about it anymore. Change the subject." I rubbed at my eyes, pushing away the urge to crawl back up to my room and hide underneath my covers.

"A'ight, well, I'll give you a game." He pointed towards the tv. "Let's race, and whoever wins - best of three - has to go out and buy a shit load of junk food."

"What for?" My brows furrowed in confusion.

"Cause I really, really want some chocolate right now. Like, lots of it. And crisps. And coke. God, I need some coke."

"You sound like you're about to have an orgasm over the thought of drinking soda," I laughed, watching him with bemused eyes. "Besides, we have coke in the fridge."

"Is it in a can?"

"No...?"

"Bottled coke doesn't taste as nice as canned." He explained. I didn't really understand how that was possible, since it was the same shit just in different wrapping. But, that's a typical Felix thing to say.

"Okay...then," I stood up, swapping the game discs, inserting our favourite car game and handing Lee the other controller. Sitting back down, I gave Lee a look of pure confidence. "May as well but your coat on now, cause I'm gonna kick your ass."

He snorted. "Don't be too sure about that." A smirk made it's away across his lips.

Chapter 15

Mondays. I hated Mondays for obvious reasons, but this particular Monday was even worse than the rest. Today could
either destroy my whole world, or be the start of a new level of
friendship between me and Chase. You know, cause he obviously
knows I'm shagging my best friend now, and I would love him forever
he decided to keep that a secret.

I hadn't seen him yet though, but me and Lee did come early to
form today. I elbowed Lee in the side. "What about if you text him?
Get him to meet us somewhere?" I whispered. Lee rolled his eyes.

"Jake, no. We're gonna wait for him to show up here, and see if
he approaches us first, okay? And if he doesn't, then we can sneak
up behind him, throw a bag over his head and drag him off behind
west building." He said, then added as a side note, "I liked that idea
more than your other. Texting him to meet us isn't as dramatic."

"I was only joking with that one, Lee, Jesus."

"What, the kidnapping or the texting?"

"The kidnapping!"

"Really? Wow, you're getting boring on me, babe." He smirked. I sighed in irritation and let my gaze wander back over to the door to our form. An immediate surge of anxiety rushed up through my chest, and my breathing quickened. Chase had finally shown up. He didn't even try and be subtle, what with the incredibly wide eyes and the intense staring he was doing.

I gulped, trying to figure out if he wanted me to walk over to him or if that was a look of complete disgust. Or maybe it was the look of impending doom. I couldn't decide, until he nodded his head towards the doorway, indicating me to follow him. I sighed in relief, looks like it was the first.

I glanced towards Felix. "I'm scared." I whispered, looking for re-assurance, but he just shoved me away from him and told me to get on with it. I trudged my way out the room, finding Chase a little down the empty corridor, leaning against the wall on my left. I stopped by his side, propping myself against the wall too, shoving my hands in my pockets so that he couldn't see them shaking slightly.

"Hey," I said, shrugging my shoulders, trying to shake off the anxiety.

"Hey," He smiled at me, an awkward, nervous smile. "I wanted you to know that, yeah, I was a bit freaked out I mean," he chuckled. "You know, two of my best friends makin' out behind west building, both of them got dicks, am gonna be a little shocked, right? But it's cool. Am cool with it. And I ain't gonna tell nobody, not unless you want me to." He seemed to breathe a sigh of relief once he'd finished speaking. I joined in with him.

"So you don't hate me? You're not disgusted with me? You haven't told a single soul? Have you? Have you told anyone? No one knows, right?" I whispered furiously. Despite everything he'd just said, I was growing increasingly more panicked by the second.

"Woah, woah, Jake, man, chill out." He held his palms up in front of me. "I haven't said a word. I don't hate you, and even if I did I definitely wouldn't be disgusted. Man, what d'you take me for, homophobic? I ain't as low as that. I'm insulted." He shoved my shoulder playfully, a smile playing about his lips.

"Oh my god it feels like Christmas has come early," I felt my whole body relax as I exhaled. "Jesus shit, Chase, you scared the fuck out of me all weekend. I thought, well, I thought we were done, man."

"Nah, man. As long as you don't go doin' your thing with your new boyfriend all up in my face, we cool. Cause I don't need'a see that action. I like my ladies, you know, I don't wanna get converted. And this guy," he pointed down to his crotch. "Well he's easily influenced."

I raised my eyebrows at him. "Don't tell Lee that, he'll fuck with you all day. Metaphorically. Obviously." I paused for a moment, deep in thought. "Actually...no, if you gave him the chance he'd probably fuck you for real."

"Aren't you guys, like, going out or somethin' though?" Just as Chase said that, the hallway flooded with students leaving the form room, all of them heading off to first period. The sound of teenage banter filled the small area.

"Yeah," I replied. "But, I don't know, maybe he'll get bored of me and wanna try someone else?" Chase's eyebrows furrowed. He opened his mouth to speak, but his words were silenced as Lee huddled in with us against the wall, braving out the stampede of people passing through the narrow corridor.

"So are we lovers or haters?" Lee shouted above the noise.

Chase replied for me. "Lovers, man. Always lovers." He grinned. Lee fist pumped the air.

"See I told you, Jake. I told you he'd be cool with it."

"Yeah, yeah," I waved a hand in his direction, brushing him off. "Come on, we better head to class."

Ah, English. English. English. English. I fucking hated this class. But I did get to sit next to Bonnie in this lesson, as apparently we'd assigned ourselves our own seats, which were always right next to each others whenever we had class together. I mean come on, who wouldn't wanna sit next to Bonnie Tyler? She could turn a gay man straight. But I was already straight, I just...liked to shag Felix. It– it made sense in my head, okay?

This time we were sat at a four-seated table, Bonnie was right at the end, I was on her right and on my right sat Felix, who was leaning forward on his elbows giving Bonnie a very weird glare. Whenever she would directly look his way, however, he would give her a very weird smile. I didn't really know what to make of it, to be honest. Neither did Bonnie, by the looks of it.

"So I never did get that call," she murmured in a light, playful voice. "I was free all weekend."

"Ah, yeah, sorry. Had my hands full." I almost choked at the imagery that flooded my mind at my words. "I mean, I, uh. I had a lot of stuff to do...for my father. Around the house."

Bonnie slowly nodded her head. I think she caught on to the fact that I'd made that up. "Well if you're free next weekend, maybe you could come get your hands full around my house?" She winked, laughing quietly.

It was then that I got nudged in the side by Lee's elbow, a little too much strength behind the action than was needed. He tapped his pen on the side of my page, pointing towards a tiny drawing of a dick.

I wasn't sure if he'd done it just as a joke, because it really was a very "Lee" thing to do, or if there was more to it than that. Lee always did get jealous easily. It wasn't like I was doing anything wrong? I wasn't the one flirting here, Bonnie was.

It went on like that throughout the entire lesson. Bonnie would make some flirty remark or innuendo and then Lee would do something to steal my attention away from her and so on and so forth. I felt like they were playing tug of war and I was the rope. It made me slightly pissed at Felix, though. Did he have to be so controlling? Could I not even talk to girls any more?

Finally the lesson came to an end and I stormed out of the classroom without saying a goodbye to Bonnie. Although I did spare a second to flip Lee the middle finger as I charged out the door. He wasted no time in catching up to me in the hallway. He pulled me close to him, holding me tightly by the arm as he walked, whispering furiously into my ear.

"You asked me out, Jake, not the other way round. So start acting like a fucking boyfriend and not a two-faced, cheating whore." He released his grip on me after he'd spat those words into my ear. They made my whole body stall momentarily, my mind fumbling with the controls and trying to figure out just how to get my legs to work again.

"Felix!" I shouted after him, finally able to move again. He was shoving his way through the oncoming traffic of people, not caring who he pushed out of the way. "Felix, come on. Wait. We need to talk!" He spun around on his heels.

"Do we? Do we really, Jake?" I was confused at the question. I suspected he was trying to accuse me of something but I couldn't quite figure out what. "We always need to talk whenever you wanna talk, don't we? It doesn't matter when I want to, though. Right?" He sighed. "You know what, fuck it. I don't know. I'm out of here." He turned back around, starting off towards the building's entrance. I followed closely behind him.

The next time I spoke was just after we'd left the premises of the school. "Lee, where are we going?" He didn't reply, just upped his pace like he was trying to get away from me. Hell, he probably was. But we really did need to talk about this.

I needed to explain everything. I wanted to be the guy he wanted me to be, I just...that would mean changing everything about me. I was flirty, I was arrogant, I hung around with a lot of girls. To be who Lee wanted me to be, would mean changing that. I wasn't sure if I really wanted to.

Eventually Lee's power walk came to an end inside an empty bus shelter. The atmosphere was quite dull thanks to the grey clouds in the sky, but I wasn't gonna let that dim my determination to say what I needed to say.

"Look, I'm sorry, okay? I'm sorry for being the way I am. You've always been fine with it before, but now you want me to change? I'm not sure if I can do that for you, Lee."

"Are you kidding me?" He glared at me. "Jake I'm not asking you to reinvent yourself. I'm asking you to be faithful."

"I haven't even cheated!"

"No but you will!" He shouted, throwing his hands in the air. "You will. Won't you? Don't lie to me, Jake. I know the answer is yes. I know it is because I know you."

"So if you know me so well, then why did you ever agree to go out with me in the first place? Apparently you're saying it's inevitable that I'm going to cheat on you, so why say yes?"

"Because I love you. I fucking love you. I couldn't have said no even if I'd really wanted to."

He sat down on the metal bench that ran along the glass bus shelter, and dropped his head into his hands. His fingers buried themselves in his blonde hair. I knelt down in front of him, pulling his hands away from his face. He looked at me with red rimmed eyes.

"I'm sorry." I was full of sincerity. I don't think I'd ever been more sincere in my life. "I'm sorry that you have this real shitty expectation of me, but I'm gonna do everything I can to prove you wrong. I'm not gonna cheat on you, Lee. I'm sorry that I flirt and like to hang around with girls and, you know, I guess I do stare quite a bit, but I do it without realising a lot of the time but I'll try to stop, okay? I'll try to stop just, don't be pissed at me."

"I just feel like you're trying to prove something. Maybe to yourself, maybe to others, I don't know. I just feel you're trying to prove that you're not gay, so that you don't feel different. Do you know what I mean?"

"I'm not gay–" Lee groaned, pulling his wrists out of my grip and standing up.

"Jesus Christ, when are you going to admit it? You are gay, Jake. Whether you like it or not. Maybe not exclusively, sure, I can believe that from the way you eye-rape Bonnie every time she walks into your line of sight. But you can't deny that you're gay when you have a boyfriend."

I sighed, shaking my head. I didn't want to talk about this any more. We weren't exactly getting anywhere. My eyes were growing more and more tired with every second and I wanted nothing more than to be able to crawl into my bed and sleep the rest of the day away.

"I'm done talking about this." I said, heading out the shelter. As I was walking away, I turned back to say over my shoulder, "I'll prove you wrong, you know." Whether it was proving I wouldn't cheat, or proving I wasn't gay, I wasn't entirely sure.

Lee didn't reply, so I left without another word.

Chapter 16

W e returned to school after our fight at the bus shelter, but when we passed in the corridors or was in the same class, we didn't talk. He didn't even return my stares. It was once we got back to my house that I realised how pissed with me he really was. I couldn't understand why. I really didn't know what I'd done that was so bad.

He was shoving all of his clothes back into his duffel bag. He didn't care for folding, just rammed them all in there and hoped it'd fit. I followed him to and from different areas of the room as he picked up discarded clothing and his toiletries from the bathroom.

"Would you please hold up and give me a reason for why you're leaving?" I'd been asking him ever since he started packing, but he hadn't said a word until now. I fought the urge to unpack his clothing in spite of him.

"I think we need some space."

I stopped in the middle of my room. My eyes continued to trail around after his movements. "Some space." I murmured. "We're taking a break?"

"If that's how you want to look at it." His voice was continuously low and lacking in any and all of his usual enthusiasm and energy.

"I don't understand exactly; why are we going on a break? Do I not get a say in this or is it just whatever you decide?"

"Jake, don't even– just don't even start with that." He put his hand up in frustration. "I'm not in the mood to talk to you right now, okay? I need some space to figure things out in my head."

"You mean to figure out if I'm worth the effort or not."

"Jake," he sighed, irritation ringing crystal clear in his tone.

"No, no don't try and lie about this. That's the truth, isn't it? I'm not worth it, am I?"

This caused Lee to stop in the middle of my room, too, and face me directly for the first time since we got back. "I just don't want to put so much into someone who inevitably realises this wasn't ever anything real, but an experimentation. Something to try out. I don't want to be one of your little projects, Jake."

"What in the fuck made you think you were an experiment?"

"The fact that you hardly try! You just...you're all sex and, and hiding and I just I don't know, Jake. I don't know. Maybe you should figure out if this– if I am really what you want. Maybe having some time to think will be good for you too."

I didn't reply. I couldn't. I stood there with my lips in a fine line as he finished packing the rest of his stuff and he slung his duffel bag over his right shoulder. The doubt started creeping in as his words began to circulate around my mind.

Maybe he was right. Maybe I wasn't taking things seriously. Did I really want to be with Lee? Could I really see myself being in a full-on relationship with him, and telling all my friends? Is that what I wanted? I'd never really thought about it.

Having not said anything, Felix must have assumed I had nothing more to say and walked past me in silence, heading for the door.

"I don't want you to leave, Lee," my voice was dry and rough as I spoke. I heard his footsteps come to a pause. I wasn't facing him, and I didn't dare look over my shoulder. Though just as I was about to work up the courage to do so, I heard his footsteps resume and when I finally turned to look at him, he was gone.

I collapsed down onto my bed, and for the better part of twenty minutes I lay there staring up at my ceiling. There wasn't anything important going through my mind. I wasn't thinking about what had just happened between me and Lee. It was more things like remembering those little toys I used to get in cereal boxes. And the snap, crackle and pop packets I used to get with my Rice Crispies.

That was until I remembered Bonnie's offer and that she'd told me she was still waiting on that phone call. I guess now was probably the best time do that, since me and that wanker was on a break and I needed a little bit of distracting.

It took me another thirty-odd minutes to decide whether or not I wanted to meet up with Bonnie, but eventually I sent the text and now here we were, wandering through the streets with hot chocolates in hand. We'd spent the past hour in a cafe sharing chips but now we were heading down towards a local park, where we could sit at a bench and finish our drinks.

We didn't talk for a few moments and it was a little awkward, if I was honest. I took a sip of my hot chocolate, letting my eyes wander around the park, from the tall trees that towered around the outline, to the wide space of grass that we were facing.

"So how come you were so bored you had no other option than to call me?" Her words were playful, but obviously fishing for some sort of reassurance that I wanted to be here with her.

I almost replied with my boyfriend's being a little shit, but managed to stop myself and in turn said, "Trust me, you weren't a last resort, Bonnie." I smiled at her through the lie, tossing my empty hot chocolate cup in the bin beside me. "I would have called you sooner, but I've been a little busy."

She smiled, looking down at her hands which were entwined around her cup, thumbs gently moving over the polystyrene. "I'm glad you called. We should do this again sometime."

"Oh yeah, definitely." I was surprised at how well I managed to fake my enthusiasm at the idea. She was a great girl, sure, but she wasn't...I thought long and hard about this, but the truth is, she wasn't Lee. And that's all that mattered, really. This would have been a thousand times better if I was with Lee.

Bonnie nudged my thigh with her knee. I looked over at her to find a small smile playing about her lips. The beanie she was wearing made her face look small and thin, and matched the colour of her eyes that looked mahogany in the orange glow of the street lights. She was all snuggled up in her long winter coat that tied at the waist. It all made her look very delicate, which was misleading because delicate was something she most definitely wasn't.

"I should probably get home," she said quietly. "Walk me back?" I nodded, standing up and offering her my hand to help her to her feet. She was wearing very tall heels, and throughout tonight she'd been a little wobbly and unsteady on her feet. She took the opportunity to link her arm through mine to use me for support as she walked.

I didn't really mind, although it was obviously a hint that this meet up meant a little more to her than it did to me. She huddled up against my side as we slowly walked back to her house. We talked back and forth about school and the future, a bit of banter went on until we reached her house, and then her hand slid down my arm to link with my fingers as she pulled away.

"Thank you for tonight, I had a really great time." She smiled and I returned it. I didn't really see what was so great about it. All we did was talk and eat chips.

She crowded in close again and leaned in to give me a gentle, chaste kiss on the lips. I'd closed my eyes as she did, and when I reopened them I was greeted with a very prominent blush glowing on each of Bonnie's cheeks.

I probably shouldn't have given her so many compliments tonight or something. Shit, who was I kidding? I came out with the intention of flirting in the effort to try and get Lee out of my head and figure out what the fuck I really wanted. It didn't seem to be Bonnie. I felt bad for saying that after what just happened.

I never wanted to endure the wrath of Bonnie, she could be pretty damn scary when she was pissed off. I was definitely going to regret this when it finally came to the time where I had to tell her I wasn't interested. Oops?

"Okay, well, I'm gonna go," she laughed. "I'll see you at school tomorrow. Night." She let go of my hand and headed up the steps and into her house. I waited until she closed the door behind her before walking away in a somewhat dazed state.

Probably should have said something there. I didn't dwell on it too long as it's not like I had a time machine and could turn back the clock and change it, so I simply shrugged it away and decided to cross that bridge when I came to it.

I didn't fancy going home yet, so I walked around aimlessly for another hour or so, getting lost in my thoughts. Like about how much of a drama queen Felix had been lately. Fucking putting us on a break just because I checked Bonnie out in class. Seriously, he should have been born with a vagina.

He hardly ever bothered to give me an explanation for why he was pissed, apparently he just expected me to know, like I could read his mind. I don't know how he could even expect that since he was so damn cryptic. Always secretive and a god damn hypocrite, as well. He really fucking was. I was too tired to give out bullet points on why, but he was.

I twirled my phone around in my hand, contemplating whether or not to give him a text. Maybe he'd cooled down. Jesus, I sounded like a clingy girlfriend. I wasn't used to this at all. I hated it when Felix was pissed at me, but that hardly ever happened. I mean we had our little fights but they were just small, petty things that were forgotten about in the next ten minutes.

Oh fuck it, I had to sort this out. I decided I was just gonna go straight over to his house and have it out with him. The suspense was fucking killing me and I was done with this whole space and waiting it out bullshit. I liked him. A lot. I just wasn't sure if I loved him. What even is love? Does it even exist or is just an illusion people like to believe in? Something to base their happiness on. How was I supposed to know? I was still only young.

I walked the distance to his house, it only took about twenty minutes before I was there and, wasting no time, knocking on the door. When no one answered, I tried the handle and came to find that the door was unlocked. I walked inside. This wasn't the first time I'd welcomed myself into the Towson's household unannounced.

I heard some sort of sobbing or snivelling coming from the lounge, so I slowly made my way in that direction instead of up the stairs. They didn't sound like the kind of noises Felix made when he was crying, so I assumed it was his mum since she recently found out her husband was cheating on her and everything. But I was surprised to find it was actually Felix's older sister, Kim.

I stood awkwardly in the doorway, tapping my fingers on my thighs. I didn't know whether to sit down and comfort her and ask her what was wrong or whether to just leave her to it. Her body jumped as she saw me, muttering, "Jesus you scared me," in a small voice as she wiped at the mascara stains trailing down her cheeks.

"Sorry, I, um, was looking for Felix…"

She took a deep breath, her bottom lip beginning to tremble again. "God, I'm a mess," she said, still wiping at her eyes. Her voice was a deep tremor of sadness. I couldn't help myself, I'd had a crush on her since I was like five, there's obviously some part of me that cares about her.

I sat down beside her on the sofa. "What's happened?"

She combed her fingers through her hair and pulled the strands from her face that had stuck to her cheeks from her tears. "I like this guy and we hooked up and I thought we had something but then I realised I was just another name on his list of fucks, and I sound like such a stupid bitch for ever thinking I was something more to him in the first place but I just really like him, you know?"

"Oh." I cleared my throat. What was I supposed to do? Should I pat her on the shoulder? Make her a sandwich? Call the guy a dick and say she could do better? Yeah, no, instead I kinda just sat there awkwardly with my hands in my lap as she cried some more.

"I just...wanted...to have a boyfriend." She sobbed in between deep breaths and occasional pauses as she wiped at her nose and eyes.

"Hey, trust me, boyfriends aren't all they're cracked up to be." I said without thinking. I took a double-take of what I'd just said and hoped she'd been too busy wrapped up in her thoughts to have heard me properly.

But apparently not as she stopped her outrageous sobbing and turned to look at me in confusion. "You're kidding, right? They take you to the movies, tell you they love you, buy you flowers for gods sake!" Her bottom lip started shaking, and she bit down on it seemingly in an effort to hold back another wave of cries. "All my friends have them."

"Uh," I looked around the room, wishing I hadn't gotten myself involved with weird teenage chick drama. I made a mental note to bring Lee up on the fact that I hadn't received any flowers from him yet. Nor has he taken me to the movies. How dare he call himself my boyfriend and not stick to the apparent boyfriend code.

At that moment, Kimberly fell against my side, her forehead resting on my shoulder, probably wiping her mascara all over my shirt. I put my palm on her back and, not knowing what else to do, said, "There, there," in the most comforting voice I could muster. I wasn't so good with this stuff when it came to girls.

She eventually stopped crying and sat upright once more. She spent a few moments composing herself before she started speaking to me again. "Sorry about all that, Jake."

"No worries. I should probably get goin–"

"Guys can be real dicks, you know?" She cut in, stopping me from making my swift exit which I needed to make pretty soon if I wanted to keep my sanity. "I hope you're not one of those kinda guys, Jake."

I gulped. "Course not." She looked at me, although it didn't really feel like she was seeing me. "Why guys would, erm, ever treat a girl like that...you know, it's just disgusting." I rambled. My eyes kept drifting over towards the door. I was hoping she wasn't going to have another break down again. I'd like to keep my white shirt white, thank you very much.

She leaned in towards me again, but this time she didn't go for my shoulder, she went for my lips. I sat there in stun as her mouth pressed against mine. As her lips started moving and her hand came up to wrap around my neck, my mind started racing a mile a minute.

This was the girl I'd had a crush on since forever. This was the girl I'd always wanted to hop to it with but she'd always seen me as some little boy. I was kissing Kimberly Towson. This was like my thirteen year old self's dream.

Just as she pulled away I heard words that hadn't come from my own mouth, and they were far too deep to come from Kim's that said, "Hey I'm just going to go down to the store to..." they trailed off just as my eyes trailed from Kim's face to the doorway to find Lee standing there, disbelief all over his face.

"Are you kidding me?" I didn't hear anger in his tone. I didn't hear anything but what sounded like exhaustion. Like he just didn't have any energy to show his anger or his sadness. And that, somehow, was worse.

I looked towards Kim and back to Felix, wordlessly. I had no idea what I could say in this situation to flip the coin and make Felix believe it wasn't what it looked like. Kimberly was watching in a sort of blank confusion, not fully understanding what was so wrong, why tears were welling up in Lee's eyes and why I was desperately trying to search for an excuse.

"Lee, please–" I forced my legs to stand up, they felt shaky beneath the weight.

My movements seemed to have kicked Lee's head into gear as he shook his head and walked away whilst saying, "Whatever, man, I'm so done with this."

"What have I got in between?" Kimberly asked, still sitting on the sofa. I glanced down at her, feeling a deep pang of guilt in the pit of my stomach.

"Nothing. Just...nothing." I murmured before leaving to chase Felix outside the front door. He was already half way down the path and I had to run to catch up to him.

"Don't bother saying a word, Jake." My feet had pounded so heavily on the concrete that he knew I was right behind him as I slowed to a walk. I was breathing as though I was badly out of shape, but really it was more the panic I was feeling that was causing my breathing to be so loud and fast.

"Felix you gotta hear me out. I came round to see you–"

"I don't give a fuck, Jake!" He spun on his heels, jolting me in my steps. "That was my sister! My fucking sister! I know you've had the hots for her since you were a kid but are you fucking serious? Hell, I'd have taken you cheating with Bonnie over you cheating with her. Of all fucking people, you sick bastard."

"Okay, wait, just chill a second, alright? I haven't cheated, Lee. It was just a kiss, and it didn't mean anything."

"Bullshit it didn't mean anything. All you could ever talk about was kissing her when you were twelve–"

"Thirteen," I corrected.

"I don't give a flying fuck how old you were. The point of it is that you don't take whatever this is between us seriously. You don't want to, do you? You're just not cut out for relationships. I always knew you weren't. I don't know what I was thinking getting involved with you and now look what's happened. We're fighting. I can't stand to look at you without getting this pain in my chest and it hurts so damn much, Jake."

"I'm sorry," I whispered, looking down at the pavement. I couldn't look him in the eye.

He sighed, lowering his voice back to where it sounded tired and empty. "I think it's a little late for apologies. Now I'm gonna walk away. Don't follow me.

And he did. He walked away, and I stood exactly where I was and watched him. I think I understood then what kind of pain he was talking about, cause deep in my chest I got this heavy feeling right where I felt my heart beating, that slowly tightened as though someone had reached in and enclosed their hand around my heart and was slowly crushing it. I felt sick, and all I could do was stand there.

Chapter 17

I dragged my feet all the way home, making scraping noises against the pavement which my mother would have scolded me for if she were here. I didn't care if I scuffed up my trainers. It was a long walk home but I needed it. I needed the time to clear my head, and once I finally got to my house, I headed straight for the sofa and sunk into it with a deep sigh.

Mandy joined me a few moments later. She must have heard me slam the door shut. She stood leaning against the doorway that lead to the kitchen, just staring at me in silence until she eventually said, "Right, tell me what's wrong." And collapsed into the sofa beside me.

When I didn't reply, she nudged me with her elbow. I glanced up at her, giving her a solemn smile.

"I screwed things up with Felix," I muttered, looking back down at my hands which were playing with the hem of my shirt.

"And how's that, then?" She relaxed back into the cushions as though she was getting comfortable for a long story. I shook my head. She leaned in closer and softened her voice, "Come on, you can tell me."

"I'm just an ass, that's all."

She scoffed. "Jake, honey, everyone's an ass. I doubt things are that bad between you two. You've been best friends since before I can remember. You'll sort things out, I'm sure." Her words were warm and I really wanted to let them convince me they were true but the thing is, I was pretty damn sure they weren't.

"I can't...understand why he's so angry at me. Mandy, I–" I sighed in defeat. I couldn't tell her that I was dating my best friend and now we're on a break all because I was flirting with a girl that practically meant nothing to me. I mean hell, Mandy probably already knew about me and Lee, she has hinted at the notion a few times that's for sure, but I still couldn't out-rightly say it.

But this was Mandy for Christs sake. I used to be able to tell her anything and everything, and I know she wouldn't judge me or shame me for liking a boy. I think it's the pure fact of saying it out loud to someone who I see as pretty much a mother figure. I guess would mean that I was admitting it to myself...that I was...well, that I was gay? Bisexual? See, I still wasn't even sure.

I wasn't sure if I liked guys, or if I just liked Felix. You know, maybe between me and Lee it was a sort of demisexual type thing. After all, I haven't found myself being attracted to any other guys. I haven't checked any of my other mates out. I sighed in frustration, digging my fingernails into my palms.

Just say it, Jake. Just say it.

"Mandy, I think I might be gay." I forced the words out, keeping my eyes focused on the tapping of my foot against the carpeted floor. It was silent for a moment, and I began to panic. I didn't want to look over to my left and find Mandy looking at me with disgust or, or resent, so I kept my eyes down and wondered if I'd made a mistake in confessing something that's been eating away at me ever since the first time me and Lee kissed.

"I knew you liked the D. Your father owes me fifteen quid." She said in a rather proud way. What she'd said threw me off my game and I just sort of stared blankly at the wall opposite me for a good few minutes, before I slowly turned to look at her with that same blank look.

"I'm sorry, what?"

"Oh come on, Jake! You really think we didn't know?" She was smiling; probably at the fact that a blush was slowly sneaking it's way into my cheeks.

"You made a bet with my dad over whether or not I was gay? Are you serious right now?" If my eyebrows could have, they'd have shot right off the top of my forehead leaving scorch marks behind.

"No, psh, course not. We were already pretty damn certain about that. We made a bet over whether you and Felix were," she wiggled her eyebrows. "You know, doing the...naughties." She lowered her voice to a whisper for the last word.

I immediately went back to staring blankly, with a slight bit of shock pushing it's way into my features, at the wall. "Hang on a minute," I turned back to look at her. "Who said anything about me and Lee doing the, you know, " I raised my eyebrows, not exactly wanting to say the word and repeating what Mandy had called it just seemed ridiculous. I mean, come on, the naughties? It sounds like we're thirteen again.

Mandy laughed. "It's not hard to put two and two together, hon."

"Pfft," I waved my hand at her in dismissal, shaking my head at the same time, but for a different reason. "I can't believe my dad– I thought he'd be disappointed in me or something. I thought he'd kick my ass out."

Mandy chuckled. "He'd never do that, and he'd be offended if he ever found out that you thought he would. Now, your mother on the other hand...I doubt she'll be as pleased as your father was."

"He was pleased?" Okay now the shock was definitely evident in the way my voice broke on that last word. "Oh my fucking god. How long have you guys been gossiping about this behind my back?"

Mandy shrugged innocently. "I've kinda had suspicions for a while. I mean you and Lee have never been subtle about your flirting, have you?" She winked.

"We never flirted," I muttered in annoyance.

"Oh, you did! You guys were always giving each other those sultry gazes and making little flirtatious remarks!"

"Shut up, Mandy." She hit me round the back of my head with the tea towel she had in her hand, clearly insulted. "I can't believe you guys." I muttered, finding it hard to wrap my head around the fact that my dad was totally cool with this whole situation.

"So now that we have that over and done with, what're the grimy details about why Felix is angry with you?"

"Over and done with? This is in no way anywhere near over and done with. My dad thinks I'm gay, Amanda! You guys made a freaking bet over whether or not me and my best friend were sleeping together and the fact that you're all so laid back about it all is freaking me the fuck out!"

"Yeah, yeah," she waved me off. "Now tell me about the interesting stuff. What's happened with Felix?"

I stared at her with wide, disbelieving eyes. "You're fucking crazy," I said in a breathy, confused voice. "You're all fucking mad." My eyes found comfort staring back at the wall, it almost felt like it took me out of the situation. Like I wasn't really here. If I stared at it long enough, my eye sight turned blurred and out of focus, like I'd dazed out of reality.

I was jolted out of that serenity as soon as Mandy nudged me and said, "Well, are you going to tell me or not? Maybe I can help."

I sighed. "I don't know where to begin. I guess...me and Lee decided to start dating and then I was checking Bonnie out in class one day and he just flipped a shit on me and now he's decided we're going on a break and he wants me to think about whether or not I take this thing between us seriously, or if I'm just looking for some fun, or using him as an experiment or some bullshit and then I ended up kissing his sister when I went around his house looking for him and now he's really, really pissed at me."

Mandy blinked at me in silence a few times before opening her mouth, closing it and then opening it again. "Okay, right, I think I got all that. You talk so fast sometimes, Jake, it's hard to understand you."

"Sorry," I muttered, looking off to the side. My hands were clasped together in my lap so tightly I could barely feel them.

"I think what you need to do is have a long, hard, think about whether you really are serious about you and Felix. Do you want to be with him? Or do you think this is just the curious side in you that wants to try something new? Because it's normal, Jake. For a lad your age to be curious about these things, but playing with someones feelings isn't fair."

"Yeah," I murmured beneath my breath. "How will I know? That I'm serious about it." I looked at her like she was my own personal soothsayer. Like she held all the answers, she could tell me the things I needed to hear so that I'd make the right choice. Like she knew my future, knew what I wanted, and just had to point me in the right direction. If only.

"You'll know," she smiled at me. It was the sort of smile you'd expect to come from a mother, but then I guess Mandy was sort of a mother to me. She'd been there for me a hell of a lot more than my actual mum, which was sad really.

She put her hand on my shoulder and held my gaze for a moment, still smiling that motherly smile. Then she stood up to leave, heading back towards the kitchen. It was only a few seconds after that I was racing up the stairs, deciding that I was going to lock myself in my room for the rest of the night and hide beneath my covers to think.

Gay. It was strange saying that word. Not so much saying it as it was calling myself it, really. I'd always had it in my head that I was going to marry some girl and have a family, work in an office to support them and all that boring adult stuff. That's what my mum had always told me.

I was to grow up to be just like my father. Minus the drug addict part that happened a few years ago, but that was in the past. At least, I hoped it was. From the way he's been acting lately, I was a bit hesitant to believe that. Mind you, living with a woman like my mother, I didn't really blame him for going off the deep end. She could drive anyone to madness.

The thought of my future had always been a dull one, but apparently it was becoming even more so every time I thought about growing up to be with anyone but Lee. Maybe that was what Amanda meant when she said I'd know. Whenever I thought of a future without Lee, it didn't feel all that exciting.

I pulled my duvet up over my head and curled my knees up to my chest, after digging my mobile from my trouser pocket. I held it tightly in my left hand and closed my eyes as if I could psychically make Felix call me. I scrolled to his name in my contacts a few times, but I could never push myself to press the call button.

So instead I just lay there in the dark with my phone in my hand and my duvet over my head, until eventually I drifted off into sleep.

Chapter 18

Last night was one of those nights that I spent tossing and turning, unable to rest because of the amount of thoughts racing through my mind. I guess I was sort of glad it was over, but at the same time I really wished I could rewind back to the beginning of the night so I had another nine or so hours of darkness. I wasn't quite ready for the sun to rise and the day to start, which was only about an hour or so away.

I was laying on my back, staring up at my ceiling that looked miles and miles away in the darkness of my room. It was as if I was looking straight up into a star-less space; a black canvas that shifted subtly, causing my eyes to strain and move in and out of focus.

That was, until I heard the glide of my door against the carpet and watched as orange light flooded my ceiling in a triangular shape that slowly grew wider and wider, engulfing more of the room in this soft glow of light. I tilted my head up to see who was there. At first all I could make out was a black silhouette, but the closer they came the more I could make out the familiar facial features.

My dad had this real distinct nose. It was narrow and came to a sharp point, slightly crooked towards the tip. As he sat down on the edge of my bed, the light that leaked into my room from the hall revealed half of his face, leaving the other shadowed.

"Everything okay, dad?" I asked, voice raspy.

"Yeah," he whispered in this unusually soft tone that sounded fond, almost. "I was just coming by to see how you were before I got busy with getting ready. Amanda told me you had a very honest talk with her last night, and that apparently there was something you wanted to say to me?"

I inwardly rolled my eyes. God damn woman getting me into awkward situations that I could live without. "I don't know what she was talking about. You know Mandy, she's getting old, her head is all," I pointed to my forehead and waggled my finger, insinuating she was losing it.

"Jake, don't be rude." He scolded.

I groaned, rolling my eyes as I cursed Mandy's name. "Did she tell you that you owe her fifteen quid?" I massaged my forehead with nervous fingers, trying to push away the awkwardness.

"Yes." There was a slight nod as he spoke.

"Then I think you already know what I'm s'posed to say, don't you." It wasn't a question but a statement. From the look in his eyes I could tell he knew exactly what I had to say, especially when they lowered, not able to look directly at me. Whether that was because he felt embarrassed or ashamed, I wasn't sure.

"Look, son, I know I'm not the best father and I've not been a great role model or someone to look up to, but," he paused, probably searching for the right words. These kind of speeches didn't come naturally to him. To be honest, it felt pretty unnatural to be on the receiving end of it. "I want you to feel comfortable to come to me when you need advice, or when you need help or even just to talk. About...teenage stuff. I was a young lad once, too, you know. I had...confusing feelings and–"

"Dad," I interrupted, hauling myself up into an upright position. "Me, you and these kind of talks don't really go well together." I was smiling as I said it. I didn't mean it offensively. "We're just two awkward sods when it comes down to it."

He nodded, agreeing. "Alright, that's true." He chuckled quietly. "Just, I want you to know that no matter what, I will always love you. I know, I know," he put his hands up in surrender. "That's a cheesy thing to say and I don't want to embarrass you but it's true. It'll never be any different. No matter what." He stressed the last few words. I knew what he was getting at.

"Thank you." I said in the most sincere voice I'd ever heard myself speak in. I didn't know what else to say or how to react. He's never said anything like this before, and it was really fucking great to be finally hearing it. "Thank you." I whispered for a last time.

He nodded once, looking me in the eye for a short moment before patting his knee awkwardly and standing up. "I'll see you when I get home tonight. Get some sleep, you've got a few hours yet."

"Hey dad!" As he was turning to walk away I had the sudden urge to ask the question that was still playing on my mind, since my talk with Mandy. "How do you know when you love someone? Like, what made you so sure that mum was the girl you wanted to marry?"

He pursed his lips in thought before saying, "Because, when I looked at her, no matter what was going on in my life, good or bad, I knew as long as I had her, everything would be okay. I didn't need anything else in my life to be happy. She was my happiness, and she always will be."

I guess that was the moment it hit me, really. That's exactly how I felt whenever I thought about Felix. As long as he was around, I didn't really need anyone else. I mean having other people would be great because, shit, a break from Felix every now and again doesn't do any harm. But when it came right down to it, if I had to choose anyone, it'd be him I'd wanna spend my life with.

I stayed in bed until I heard the door go as my parents left for work. I'd hit the over-tired stage where you felt this sort of high come over you. I was full of energy as I was getting ready for school, right up until I was walking into my first class and that's when my sleep deprivation kicked in. It was like I'd just been dragged backwards through a dozen fields at fifty miles per hour.

"Y'all right there, Jakey!" Owen shouted as he came bouncing over, Scottish accent blazing, throwing me into a hug. I groaned, my eyes half-closed. It was a fight to keep them open. Owen pulled away but kept his hands on my shoulders. "Ye look rough as hell, man." I groaned again.

With a quick scan around the classroom, I noticed Felix hadn't arrived yet.

"Ye lookin' for yer soul mate?" He teased as usual, pulling me against his side with an arm around my shoulder. He gave me a little shake, which just got me irritated, really.

"He not in yet?" I muttered, referring to Lee's absence.

"Nah, he isnee in today. Ye not 'eard?"

I looked at him quizzically. "Heard what?"

"Ah." His lips formed at a slant. "His parents a' filin' for a divorce." My eyes widened as I leaned out of Owen's hold, rounding on him.

"You shitting me? Honestly I go to fucking bed early for one night and this is what happens? Jesus. Is he okay? Have you spoken to him?"

"I would'a thought he'd 'ave rang ye first of all?"

Something heavy buried itself in my chest at the question. A sad realisation, I guess "No." I shook my head. "No he didn't."

"Maybe you oughta go see 'im, then, aye?" I stared at Owen for a moment. His eyes narrowed slightly. I didn't quite know how to take his suggestion. It felt as though he knew something. I wasn't sure what, but I wasn't sure I wanted to know right now, either.

I nodded. "Yeah, maybe I should." I tapped Owen on the shoulder in a sort of silent thank you for the idea, and set off towards the nearest exit and in the direction of Lee's house.

I arrived at his house to find the door open. Everything was silent as I shut it behind me and walked through the hall, down to the living room. As I entered, the first odd thing I noticed was a smashed vase laying against the wall by the kitchen door, on my left. It used to sit on the cabinet, that was up against the opposite wall to the kitchen doorway.

Just as I was about to go through into the kitchen, I heard a creak from the hall that had me spinning around to put a source to the sound. Turns out it was Felix creeping down the stairs with a puzzled look on his face.

"The hell are you doing here?" His voice was rough, like his throat had turned to sand paper. His eyes looked heavy and tired. Red-rimmed from the obvious crying.

I swallowed back the lump in my throat. "I came to see how you were. Owen told me about your parents..." my voice gave-way on me at that point, so I didn't try to say anything more and instead looked down at my feet.

"Yeah, well, now you know I'm doin' just fine so you can piss off now."

I locked gazes with him angrily. "Really? Cause you look far from god damn fine to me." I took a step towards him. "You know I had to find out from Owen about all this. You remember when I used to be your first choice?"

"Don't fucking start. I don't need this right now."

"I'm not starting anything."

"You started something the moment you walked through that door," he pointed down the hall towards the front door. His stance had squared up, like he was ready for a huge argument, but his words were soft and filled with exhaustion. "You think you can just walk in here and play forget for a while? Because I can't do that and to be fucking honest, I don't want to."

"Fine. Then let's sort this out for Christ's sake. I don't want to be like this with you, I can't stand it."

He sighed, dropping his head. "I just want you to go." He walked past me, sitting down in the sofa with a heavy sigh. I turned to face him, letting my back find support against the nearest wall.

"You need a friend right now. I used to be that to you, you remember that?"

"I don't want you to just be my friend, though. I want you to be my boyfriend. I want to have a relationship with you but you're just so fucking exhausting." There was no anger in the way he spoke, just a weak sadness to his voice. It was as though he barely had the energy to feel, but he was feeling, and all that sadness had made itself a home in his brown eyes.

"I'm sorry."

Felix laughed sardonically. "Yeah? Well I'm afraid saying you're sorry doesn't make it all better, sweetheart."

"Don't patronize me for fucks sake." I hissed, shaking my head and letting it fall back against the wall with a thud. I closed my eyes against the dull ache from the impact, until it faded and then I looked back down to where Lee was sat with his elbows on his knees and his hands interlinked with each other. His lips were pressed against the side of his thumbs.

I wanted to walk over there and wrap my arms around him, pull him down and just lay with him on the sofa for a while. I didn't want to speak. I just wanted to be with him in silence for a little. I wanted to be how we used to be. Now everything's so complicated and fucked. I've forgotten how we even got to this place.

"I'm sorry I'm such a fucking bastard, alright? I'm sorry I didn't treat you like we were genuinely together. I'm sorry I was being a grade-A piece of shit." I reeled off, hoping I was hitting the nail on the head with why he was angry at me.

"But I'm done with all that, Lee, I swear. I was fucking confused. I didn't know what I felt for you. I mean...I did, it was more accepting those feelings that caused me to freak out. Letting go of who I used to be was a hard fucking thing to do. You expected way too much from me. You had your time to come to terms with everything, I was still hung up over the fact that I had kissed a fucking lad weeks after it'd happened!"

The realisation that that was why I'd been acting the way I was, came right at that moment. There was nothing rehearsed about this speech. I had no idea what I was gonna say until I was saying it. And that confession just spilled out of my mouth as if it was what I'd intended to say all along.

I hoped the expression on Felix's face was that of understanding. That was the most honest I'd been about this whole situation.

"That still doesn't make up for you kissing my sister."

"But that didn't mean a single fucking thing! I came round looking for you, and she was there crying so I asked what was up and the next thing I know she's kissing me. I swear that's how it was. Nothing more. I didn't feel anything, I promise."

Lee's head had dropped into his hands, I couldn't see his face but I could hear the sound of his sniffling and watched as he tried to subtly wipe at his eyes and nose. I walked over to his side and sat down beside him, putting an arm around his shoulder for comfort.

"Hey, hey, hey, it's alright," I whispered by his ear, my forehead resting against the side of his. "Man, I'm really sorry for everything. You're going through a lot right now and I'm just making it worse. I didn't come here with the intention to fight, honest to god. I want you to know that I'll always be here for you, though. I don't want you to keep pushing me away like this."

He shook his head, peering up at me from behind his blonde fringe that was clung to his forehead. "Shit." He whispered. "Look, you shouldn't be the one saying sorry. I mean, I don't know, I guess I should be saying sorry, too." He dragged his hands down his face. "I'm just...I'm really insecure when it comes to you. I know I probably over analyzed everything you did cause, fuck, I'm scared." His voice broke on the last word.

"Scared of what?"

"Scared that you didn't really like me, I guess. Scared that I'd lose you to Bonnie, or some other girl. Jesus, when I caught you with

Kimberly I had it in my head that maybe you two had been going at it all along."

I laughed. "Seriously? Sure, I mean I did have a thing for your sister ever since I knew what a penis was for but I can definitely assure you now that I don't want any other Towson but you, Lee."

He stared at me for a moment. I wasn't sure if it was in disbelief or if he was annoyed I'd used the word penis in reference to his sister.

"Okay," he murmured, a gentle smile playing around the edges of his lips. He didn't really look like he knew what else to say. I didn't mind. I let my forehead fall against his as my hand slid up his shirt and balled into a fist at his shoulder, pulling him closer.

"You wanna start over? Do it right this time?" I asked, my hand finding the collar of his shirt.

He nodded, nudging his nose against mine once and then for a second time before he kissed my bottom lip, then my top, and before I knew it my back had hit the sofa's cushions and Lee's body was pressed against mine.

Epilogue

I let out a hefty sigh and pulled myself up for the last time, my stomach muscles burning from the exercise I'd been doing in an attempt to relieve some stress.

I'd asked Chase to join me at my house. He was the only guy I could talk to about this whole Felix situation, and I really needed someone to help me figure it out.

He was laid outstretched on my bed with my PS Vita in hand, not really paying attention to anything I'd been saying previously. But to be fair, I hadn't been saying anything of importance, just venting random shit that had been clustering up my head for a while.

"So what am I gonna do, mate?" I said finally, throwing myself across the empty space at the bottom of my bed. Chase was pretty short, which made my bed look a lot bigger than it actually was. I fought the urge to tease him every time.

"Whatever you want to." He murmured, not caring at all. I was half ready to snatch that console out of his hands and put it on top of somewhere very high, where the short ass couldn't reach it.

"Chase!" I shouted at the top of my voice, laughing as he shot upright, eyes as bright as ever.

"What the fuck is wrong wi' you? Crazy bastard. Jesus." He exclaimed, palm flat against his chest, calming himself down. "Don' you know not to disturb a guy when he's gaming?"

"If I'm not more important than a stupid game, then we're gonna have a problem." I gave him a half-arsed pissed off look from where I was laying, one side of my face squished into the covers of my bed, which probably didn't help the expression.

"Oh I'm sorry, I didn' re-a-lise we was a pair'a white chicks." He mocked.

"What has being white got to do with it?" Chase didn't reply, simply kissed his teeth, with an attitude he needed to adjust, and refocused his eyes on the console's screen. I rolled my own eyes and shoved my face into my bed sheets, regretting my choice in friends.

"If you don't start helping me," I mumbled into the covers, pausing to breathe in the sweet smell of the scented softner, that Mandy used to wash the sheets in. "I'm seriously gonna start to cry."

Chase groaned as I heard the satisfying noise of the console landing softly into my bedding, just to the right of me. I shot upright, ready and waiting his guidance.

"First of all, you gotta tell me what it is that's even goin' on, cause that ain't even been explained to me yet." He raised his thick, dark brows at me that curved smoothly into arches.

"Okay, I'm gonna give you the short and sweet version, alright?" Chase nodded. "Basically, me and Lee had a fight cause he doesn't think I'm taking things seriously, and so I went round his place a little while after to talk things through and I found Kim sitting there, sobbing over some guy, right, yeah? You keeping up?"

"Yeah I'm keeping up, carry on." He waved his hand lazily, leaning back against the pillows, hands behind his head.

"Anyway, she comes onto me, hands around my neck and everything and, of course, Lee chooses that moment to walk in and gets the completely wrong idea–"

"Ohh shit." He commented, chuckling a little.

"Dude come on," I shot him a glare which quietened him down. "Anyway we sorted that out and I explained everything to him. But the thing is, is that before I went round to his, I'd just come from hanging out with Bonnie and the reason this is a problem, is because she ended up kissing me before I left and I haven't, exactly, quite gotten round to telling Lee this...just yet."

"What is wrong wit' you? Kissin' two girls in one night and one of them bein' a crazed bitch that Lee can't even stand, and the other bein' his sister? You an idiot, you know that?"

"Yeah, I know. But it was literally just a quick, one second kiss. That's it. So, should I even bother bringing it up? Because it didn't mean anything, and I don't want to get into another fight. I'm getting pretty tired of falling out with him."

Chase leaned forward all business-like, with his lips pouted and an eyebrow arched. "A good relationship, and more importantly, friendship is one without the secrets. So you tell me what you should do." And then he relaxed back against the pillows, smiling.

"Uh..." I chewed the inside of my cheek.

"Oh Jesus Christ, Jake, you tell him! Obviously!" He shouted, throwing his arms about like he'd given up on life. And when he'd settled, he murmured a sly, "Dumb ass." under his breath.

I scowled at him. "You sure he's gonna be okay with it?"

"Hell no he ain't gon' be okay wit' it, but you fucked up, so you deserve whatever the hell you get."

"Oh thanks, Chase. You really are the greatest friend ever."

"Honesty is key," he winked, grinning far too smugly.

I rolled my eyes. "Yeah...whatever."

I left Chase laying on my bed, PS Vita back in hand. He was so focused on the damn thing, that I doubt he even noticed I'd walked out.

I'd messaged Lee, asking him to meet me at the bridge that was our special little place. The bridge that he tried to break his fists against, the night he found out his parents had it out about his dad being a cheating bastard.

I guess I wasn't much better than him, considering the reason I'd asked Lee to meet me, was to tell him that I'd kissed Bonnie. The worst part about it, was that it didn't even feel like cheating.

Lee arrived at the bridge only five or so minutes after I did. His hood was up, shielding his face, and his hands were shoved in his pockets as he shouldered the light gusts of wind. He stopped beside me, propping one foot up against the wall.

"Hey," I muttered, barely making eye contact.

"Hey," he said back in almost the same tone. It was silent for a moment, and then, "just so we're clear, I have not forgiven you. Not completely. Or at all. Okay? I just can't be bothered to fight anymore. It's gotten boring."

I nodded weakly. "It's incredible how unsurprising it is to hear you say that."

Lee smiled as he dropped his head and his hood slid even further over his face. He pushed it back, leaving his hair messy and exposed to the persuasion of the chilly evening air.

"I need to tell you something." I began. My fingers found comfort in the pockets of my trousers. "I should have told you this the other night, but I didn't want to..." I inhaled deeply, fighting the urge to replace the truth with an easy lie. "I was afraid of losing you for good, I guess."

Lee cleared his throat and shifted awkwardly beside me. "Okay."

"So, erm, I'm just gonna come out and say it, alright?"

"Yeah whatever, just get it over with."

I bit my bottom lip, trying to distract myself from the nausea that was beginning to make an appearance in the back of my throat. "I kissed Bonnie before I came round to your house the other night."

Lee stood there in silence, staring off at the river in front of us. The sound of the water running beneath us helped to calm my nerves, if only a little.

"I'm not gonna make up any excuses." I said, after Felix continued to say nothing. "But I swear to god, I will do anything you ask of me to make things right between us. I want to be with you, Felix. I really do."

I could see him chewing the inside of his cheek, but there was next to no emotions in his features. Not even a hint of sadness or anger. His expression was simply blank. And then he turned and looked me straight in the eye, with a subtle curve to his lips.

"You wanna make this right?" He asked, and I nodded eagerly, pleading him with my eyes. "Then you gotta prove it to me, one way or another. I'm not gonna tell you how. You can figure that out for yourself."

He kicked himself off from the wall and with slow movements, he slid his fingers round my neck and placed a soft kiss to the corner of my lips, before walking away.

I stood there for a long time in thought. His kiss had left me with a cold shiver. It didn't feel like a loving kiss; it felt empty and dead. I spent the rest of the night trying to think of how I could prove to him that I wanted to be with him.

It was just as the sun was rising, starting a new school day, that it clicked.

Surprisingly, I wasn't tired at all when I walked into school after having stayed up all night sitting on the bridge. I think my brain was on overdrive and after what I was going to do today, I just knew I wouldn't be sleeping again tonight.

I waited until lunch, when all my friends – and all the people who liked to chill near us to make it look like they knew us, but in reality we had no idea who they were – were all gathered around me. Lee was talking with Owen in the center of the crowd, I had Chase to converse with until I built up enough courage to do what I was going to do.

Chase had no idea what I had in mind. I did play with the idea of telling him, to see what he'd think of it. But I didn't want him to convince me to back out, cause other than this idea, I couldn't come up with any other way to drill it into Lee's brain that I genuinely was serious about us this time.

I tapped my foot anxiously against the pavement. Oh man if I didn't do it now, I wasn't ever going to. So I jumped up onto the nearest picnic table, where a few people were still eating their lunches. I apologised for standing on one of their sandwiches, but they just waved me off with a smile.

"Hey everyone, I erm," I took a deep breath, foot still tapping. "I just wanted to say something." I shouted over the noise that was rapidly getting quieter until eventually it was dead silent and everyone's eyes were watching me with close scrutiny.

"Hey," I said, awkwardly. I looked over at Chase for support, to find him making weird gestures at me which I think meant what the hell are you doing?

I smiled at him nervously. "I just wanted to make something clear to everyone, so I can feel better about myself...I guess. Or, you know, more accepting of myself."

Everyone's eyebrows furrowed at that. "See I've come to the realisation that, erm, that I like a...person," I stuttered out. My bravery was getting smaller and smaller with every stupid word that came out of my mouth.

"And that person likes me back, and I've been a bit shitty to them because, well, I was trying to understand my feelings. It took me a while but, I think I've figured it out now."

"Everyone knows how much I appreciate the female anatomy," a few people cheered and clapped at my words. A few random arms fist pumped the air. I swallowed, fearing the life of my popularity as I went on to say, "But I have also come to find that I also appreciate the male anatomy."

My eyes found Bonnie's at the back of the crowd, who had a hand over her mouth. It didn't seem to be in anything other than surprise.

"I need to apologise to a few girls, who I may have lead on purely out of keeping myself from accepting how I feel for this guy that, frankly, puts up with a lot of my shit and I'm still failing to see why."

I sought out Lee's gaze then. I could always find him in a crowd of a thousand people, and that made me smile momentarily. But what made me grin, was the plain shock that had set into his features. I was afraid it was going to become permanent if he didn't relax soon.

"So you're gay?" A voice shouted from the crowd.

"Uh, bisexual. I think. I don't know, who needs labels?" I shrugged. It was silent for what felt like eternity. All these wide eyed teenagers staring up at me was starting to make my skin crawl.

And then all of a sudden there was a loud cheer from a small group of guys somewhere in the center, which then evolved into synchronized clapping throughout the entire crowd. A few people walked away with crinkled foreheads, but I focused more on the positive.

"So who's the lucky guy?" I heard from my left.

"Yeah Jake, who's the lucky guy?" My eyes shot back to Lee who was watching me with a smug grin. I smiled at his question, dropping my head in embarrassment before looking back up at him.

"You know exactly who it is, you bastard." He smiled, hiding his eyes with his hand. People began pushing him forward through the crowd, and then continued to lift him up onto the picnic table alongside me.

There was laughter and cheering all around us, but above everything there was chatter. You just knew this was going to be spread around the school in no time.

But hey, I didn't care. It was out now. Lee was smiling again. He was smiling. The way he used to when we were together. And it was real. I missed that so much and I couldn't even explain how great it felt to see it again.

He punched me gently in the shoulder. "You're an idiot."

"What, you didn't like it?"

"No, I just didn't expect it."

I pressed my lips together to keep the smiles at bay. "You're blushing," I elbowed him, and he elbowed me back, falling into my side clumsily and almost sending us toppling off the side of the table. I managed to keep us upright, thankfully.

"You're sweating," he pointed out in return. I wiped my forehead with my sleeve.

"Do you blame me? That's the ballsiest thing I've ever fucking done!"

"Is it?" That look was back in his eyes; the playful, flirty look that darkened his features. He moved in closer, but kept his arms by his side as our faces neared collision. He angled his lips so they were positioned just slightly out of reach of my own.

"Wanna do something ballsier?" He whispered. I arched an eyebrow and smirked with one corner of my lips. The crowd went silent once they realised what was about to happen.

"Jesus Christ," my voice was ragged. I wasn't sure if I should be feeling so turned on right now, but I was. I licked my lips and let myself fall forward just enough for my mouth to collide with Lee's which soon morphed into a dirty kiss with tongue and wandering hands.

Everyone was screaming and shouting and I heard a voice above them all that sounded a lot like Chase saying, "Alright, yo, this ain't no free show! You wanna watch you gotta pay, get yo' wallets out!" It was just like him to take any opportunity he could to make some side cash.

Eventually we took a breather, laughing quietly in the space between us. Lee leaned back enough to catch my gaze. "I still don't forgive you." He deadpanned.

I shoved him off the side of the table and he fell into the crowd who caught him in time, before he crashed into the concrete. I jumped down to where he was standing. "Yeah you do." I said, voice low and content.

He paused for a moment, eyes wandering over my face. "Yeah." He smirked. "Yeah I do."